THE
PRISONER
APPRENTICE

Other books by Stephen Elboz

The House of Rats
Ghostlands
The Tower at Moonville
The Byzantium Bazaar
Temmi and the Flying Bears
Temmi and the Frost Dragon
A Handful of Magic
A Land Without Magic
A Wild Kind of Magic
An Ocean of Magic

THE
PRISONER'S
APPRENTICE

STEPHEN ELBOZ

OXFORD
UNIVERSITY PRESS

OXFORD
UNIVERSITY PRESS

Great Clarendon Street, Oxford OX2 6DP

Oxford University Press is a department of the University of Oxford.
It furthers the University's objective of excellence in research, scholarship,
and education by publishing worldwide in

Oxford New York

Auckland Cape Town Dar es Salaam Hong Kong Karachi
Kuala Lumpur Madrid Melbourne Mexico City Nairobi
New Delhi Shanghai Taipei Toronto

With offices in

Argentina Austria Brazil Chile Czech Republic France Greece
Guatemala Hungary Italy Japan Poland Portugal Singapore
South Korea Switzerland Thailand Turkey Ukraine Vietnam

Oxford is a registered trade mark of Oxford University Press
in the UK and in certain other countries

British Library Cataloguing in Publication Data
Data available

ISBN–13: 978–0–19–276334–1
ISBN–10: 0–19–276334–2

1 3 5 7 9 10 8 6 4 2

Typeset by Newgen Imaging Systems (P) Ltd., Chennai, India
Printed in Great Britain by Cox & Wyman Ltd, Reading, Berkshire

For Helena Pielichaty, fellow writer,
partner in crime, and freelance heckler

Once it had been a fine building, handsome even, with flower gardens on three sides and an orchard at the back. Then the city had expanded rapidly and it was caught out on the wrong side, the industrial side, with its hotchpotch of factories and depots and chimneys that smoked all through the day and into the night.

These days the old house stood sad and neglected at the end of a mud track off Cigarette Factory Road, its panelling and fireplaces long gone and window frames rotting—no longer a gentleman's country residence but a laundry owned by Mrs Pafnutkin and run by her crew of orphans. It was said that Mrs Pafnutkin kept orphans in the attic and pigs in the back yard, the only difference between them being that the pigs weren't expected to earn their keep.

I should know; my name is Yanis; this was where I lived.

There, I've told you my name, but don't ask anything else about me, not even what I looked like then, for at Mrs Pafnutkin's each and every one of us looked the same. Grey, thin, exhausted—as drab as ghosts in sunlight, *or* convicts. For our hair was cropped to the scalp every second Friday—even the girls'—this being the best way to keep down lice. And, like beggars, we wore our clothes until they rotted off our backs, or by some miracle or chance we managed to outgrow them and burst out at the seams. And despite the clouds of cleansing steam and the overpowering, ever-present smell of carbolic soap, we lived surrounded by dirt and squalor. You could almost watch the mould creep across the damp walls, and in dark undisturbed corners pale spindly mushrooms flourished into thriving colonies.

As for the grande dame of the place, our Mrs Pafnutkin, well, she wasn't the cruellest of people, but neither was she the brightest. You saw it at once: there was nothing behind her tiny eyes; her gaze as blank as a goat's. She was also very large, her awkward bulk supported on the tiniest of ankles. This was God's curse on her. (We knew, she told us often enough.) She was like a dancer forced to walk on her toes. Five . . . six . . . seven . . . steps and then she was done for, falling back onto a stool dutifully carried behind by a small orphan, as skilled in his work as any of us—for he had learned to leap aside the moment she dropped, as one would from the path of a landslide.

The business of cleaning other people's clothes ran from the top of the house to the bottom. On the third floor was the sorting room, below that the washing room, and below that the drying and ironing rooms. The babies slept in crates on the landings, kept warm by the steam. As for me, I was a sorter. *Yanis, the champion sorter.* I'd done the job so long I could do it with my eyes shut, feeling the difference between linen and cotton, wool and muslin, flannel and, well, whatever else you cared to name. I tell you, I was so good at my job, I could recognize different stains by my fingers too. The others laughed at me when I told them this, but I swear to you it was true.

Apart from her ridiculously dainty ankles, Mrs Pafnutkin's other great concern was the authorities. She lived in terror that someone from the Town Hall would descend on her and close the orphanage down. 'And then where shall I be . . . ? I'll tell you, shall I . . . ? Out there on the streets without a dracul to my name; *me*, who's given such service to the brats of complete strangers . . .' After a few tumblers of vodka she became particularly maudlin. She'd have us listen to her fears and hug us by the armful; and we could only shrug at each other and wonder if she could really be expecting our sympathy.

Normally it took no more than an official-looking letter to set her off, but one day Mrs Pafnutkin was more frantic than usual. She appeared in the sorting room, stool-carrying orphan in tow, and breathless from the stairs. Without a word of explanation she crossed the floor mysteriously and took up a place beside one of the tall windows at the front of the house.

I carried on working and paid her no attention until she beckoned me over.

'Yani—here, here.'

I dropped a bundle of sheets and pillow-cases, and waded over drifts of unsorted laundry.

'Take a look out there, Yani. Tell me what you see.'

Outside, week-old snow lay stale on the ground, shovelled up into dirty shapeless piles around the dried-up fountain. Further off, industrial chimneys sent clouds of orange smoke rising into a colourless winter sky. Below me, someone was stepping back as if to take in the frontage of the orphanage better.

I turned to Mrs Pafnutkin.

'A gentleman.'

'*I know that. What's he doing?*'

'Looking around . . . Looking in through the downstairs windows.'

A sob heaved through Mrs Pafnutkin's body and she fell back onto the stool, certain as always it would be there to catch her.

'Are you all right, ma'am?'

She waved her hand angrily.

'Never mind me. Look again. What's he doing now?'

'Same as before, ma'am—snooping around.'

'*Snooping*, that's right. I don't like this, I don't like this at all. He's not one of our regular customers, is he? He's not one of our usuals?'

I shook my head.

Mrs Pafnutkin's face crumpled, pink and sweaty, on the verge of tears.

'He's from the Town Hall, I just know it. When I got up this morning the tea leaves at the bottom of my cup made the shape of an axe. So I said then if this isn't a sign from God—a bad sign—I don't know what is. And now this proves I was right . . . He's from the Town Hall and has a warrant in his bag with my name on it.'

'I don't think he has a bag, ma'am.'

'*Then it is in his pocket.* Believe you me. Lord—O, Lord, why do you persecute me? Where is he now, Yani?'

'I don't know, ma'am—I can't see him.'

Trying to spot the man, we edged from window to window, which was easy to do as all the internal walls had been removed. By now the others had stopped what they were doing and come across and joined us, grinning and revelling in Mrs Pafnutkin's dramatics. As if for safety, she gathered us closely around her like a mother hen surrounded by her chicks.

Some of the bigger lads goaded her.

'What will you do if he closes you down, Mrs Pafnutkin?'

'Just think, these may be the last sheets that ever get washed here. The very last ones, Mrs Pafnutkin.'

Mrs Pafnutkin clutched her chest where she believed her heart lay.

'Yani—you take a look again. I don't think my poor old ticker can stand the strain.'

I peered around the window and there he was; he was looking a different way, so I could study him closely.

I thought him rather odd. He had the fresh face of a young man, but his clothes were old-fashioned and thrown together in such a way as to suggest he didn't much care what the world thought of him. His coat looked as if it were made to fit a far bigger man, and the same over-sized fellow must surely have once owned that mound of moth-eaten fur that sat on the stranger's head as a sorry excuse for a hat. But in terms of oddness alone, it was the man's spectacles that took the prize. They had coloured lenses. They were pink!

'Can you see? Is he holding a warrant?'

Mrs Pafnutkin was again at my shoulder, whispering in case the man might somehow overhear.

'No, but he's heading to the door.'

Downstairs we heard the doorbell jangle.

'*That's him wanting to come in,*' Mrs Pafnutkin informed us needlessly.

I could feel her fingers digging into my arm.

'Shouldn't you go and answer it?' I said.

'*What*, and let the Devil enter my own home?'

The bell rang again, this time more insistently, waking the babies in their crates on the landings. They began to cry—they were not the only ones. Falling back onto her stool, Mrs Pafnutkin let out a string of terrified sobs, which suddenly turned into a sharp intake of breath as she heard a man's voice and realized that the stranger had let himself in.

'I say . . . is anyone at home?'

Mrs Pafnutkin went rigid with fright. I unpicked her fingers from my arm and crept out onto the landing.

The man peered up at me, curiously. Neither of us spoke. Then behind his pink spectacles he blinked.

7

'So . . . there is somebody here,' he said to himself. 'I was beginning to doubt I had come to the right place. *I said I was beginning to doubt*—' He raised his voice to be heard over the angry babies.

'You from the Town Hall, mister?'

'Me . . . ? Why no.'

I turned towards the sorting room and shouted, 'Mrs Pafnutkin—he's not from the Town Hall.'

'Ask him what he wants. *Go on*—ask him.'

'What do you want, mister?'

The man cleared his throat.

'My name is Gomarus—Dr Gomarus. I am looking to take on a boy.'

Once she realized the visitor was not an official from the Town Hall, but someone ready to do business, Mrs Pafnutkin came hobbling forward, her demeanour completely changed.

'A thousand apologies, your excellency. What must you think of us? Not answer the door to you . . . What savages you must think we are. *Polya! Polya!* Where are you, girl? Give the babies their medicine and stop this uncalled for roaring!'

Sour-faced Polya appeared with the baby medicine in an old tobacco jar as crusty with ancient

8

dribbles as a church candle. Like all other medicine at the orphanage, Mrs Pafnutkin concocted it herself. She claimed its ingredients were a secret, but we all knew it was vodka and sugar-water, which Polya now expertly dripped off her little finger into each tiny throat.

The effect was almost instant. One by one the babies dropped off into a heavy drugged sleep, stirring so little, you would think they were made of wax.

'That's it. Back you go to your land of dreams, my little ones,' cooed Mrs Pafnutkin, passing their crates crammed up against the walls.

I watched her go down the stairs, her bantam-bright eyes fixed on the doctor and her hand gripping the shoulder of her little orphan follower, using him for support in place of the banisters which had been chopped down and burned many winters ago.

Out of breath and her chest heaving, she finally reached the hallway with its floor of missing and uneven tiles. Dr Gomarus removed his fur hat and nodded; Mrs Pafnutkin planted herself upon her stool, studying him thoughtfully.

'A boy, you say, your excellency? Well, this is your lucky day. Bless me if I didn't say it would turn out lucky for someone this morning when I saw what the tea leaves predicted. It was for you, your excellency, it was for you. Of course, all my boys are fine fellows, it's the care I take of them; such hard workers too. I can see no reason why we can't find you the very thing you're looking for. *Yani*—' she bellowed upstairs to me, 'fetch Tomish and Knuckles for his excellency the doctor to view.'

I smiled to myself; how typical of Mrs Pafnutkin to try to fob off the stranger with someone she had little use for. Not that Tomish could help it. He had a withered arm; and Knuckles (nobody remembered his real name any more) was as simple as a stick. He spent hours scratching marks on his arms with a broken piece of glass and had run away twice.

Still, that was the nature of business, I suppose . . . I found them both in the washing room.

'Tomish—Knuckles, old Ma Pafnutkin wants you downstairs, at once.'

'Why?' asked Tomish squinting up his eyes in alarm.

'You'll see.'

Knuckles only laughed and pretended to box with me.

'Come on, give us a hand,' I called to the others.

Gladly leaving their drudgery at the zinc washing tubs and mangles, the other orphans crowded around and jostled the two boys through the doorway and out onto the landing. There we fell

10

back, letting them go on alone. But we kept watch, the vaguely unpleasant brown light that hovered over the stairwell making us barely visible from below.

But Knuckles, he knew we were all there, watching, and he tilted back his head to grin up at us lopsidedly. Tomish held his undeveloped arm, which made Mrs Pafnutkin frown at him, narrowing her eyes. 'Stand up straight there, Tomish—don't be so much of a slouch,' she said sharply. (There was no point giving the game away *too* early.) But nothing could be done to disguise Knuckles's shortcomings: he doubled up in a fit of giggles if Dr Gomarus so much as prodded him with a finger.

The doctor was quick to make up his mind.

He sighed.

'Unfortunately, madam, neither of these boys suits my requirements.'

Mrs Pafnutkin rocked back pretending to be surprised.

'Won't suit his excellency?'

'Dear lady, let me explain how matters stand. My permit to travel east has just come through. In fact I leave first thing tomorrow, but my assistant has gone down with scarlet fever. I need someone to replace him. A boy. Someone bright and alert, who'll fetch and carry and help me with my work.'

'And . . . what exactly *is* your work, Dr Gum—'

'*Gomarus*. I am a scientist engaged in research for the government. More than that I'm not willing to say.'

Hearing the word *government*, Mrs Pafnutkin looked alarmed.

'Oh, quite so. None of my business, in any case. But I'm sure there is a boy here perfect to your every need.'

He regarded her wearily.

'I sincerely hope so, dear lady, I can't afford to delay—our passage aboard the *Ursus* is booked and paid for . . . I'm ready to offer seventy draculs for the right boy. You see, dear lady, I had to wait six months for my permit, so it's important that everything goes to plan. I have no wish to wait another six months.'

Mrs Pafnutkin blinked her eyes stupidly.

'Did you say . . . that is, did I hear you say *seventy* draculs, your excellency?'

'Seventy. Yes. Why, is something wrong?'

'Wrong, your excellency? Why no—no, not at all.' And to me lurking at the head of the stairs she hollered more raucously, '*Yani*—I know you're up there earwigging. Get your backside into motion and round up all the boys and bring them down here for'—her voice softened—'our honourable guest, the doctor.'

12

'Yes, Mrs Pafnutkin—at once, Mrs Pafnutkin.'

I cupped my hands to my mouth. 'All boys to report downstairs—Mrs Pafnutkin's orders!'

Of course this was pure showmanship, for most boys—as well as the girls—were already out on the landings and had heard Mrs Pafnutkin well enough for themselves. However, for decency's sake, they hung back a moment or two, grinning at me, before noisily surging for the stairs.

Suddenly Dr Gomarus found himself surrounded by a horde of shaven-headed, almost identical-looking youngsters, who perplexingly, at first glance, differed only in size. He took a step or two back and I could tell from his pained expression he was beginning to regret that he'd ever come to the orphanage in the first place. He held a hand to his mouth, the smell of soap and dirt an unsettling brew.

He motioned at his spectacles. 'My eyes . . . rather weak, dear lady. If I might ask the boys to step outside for a moment.'

For seventy draculs they could dance on the roof as far as Mrs Pafnutkin was concerned. She gave an approving nod and the whole circus troop of us marched outside, the girls racing for the best positions at the windows so they wouldn't miss a thing.

Outside was raw. Rawer for those in bare feet. Snow crumbs blew around the swept cobbles, and leaves rattled in the fountain.

Aware of the effect the cold was having on us, Dr Gomarus made us boys form a line, and quickly began dismissing those he did not want, asking them to stand back against the wall. Soon I was one of only five who remained. The doctor ordered us to close up the gaps in our ranks and then began a more detailed inspection—going over each of us in turn as a farmer would a horse at market. He peered deep into our mouths; put his palm against our foreheads as if to feel how flat or angled they were. He studied our ears, eyes, and noses, and spread his fingers over our heads, probing for bumps and measuring the spans of our skulls. Behind his back, Mrs Pafnutkin shrugged in bewilderment.

At last it was down to me and Pyotr, a big blond boy whose hands and feet were so massive they made you stare. As usual, Pyotr looked down at the ground and blushed. *He* wouldn't be any use to Dr Gomarus, I decided. Not like me. For suddenly I had a desperate and overwhelming desire to be the doctor's boy and go east with him, wanting more than anything to put the orphanage and the years I had spent here behind me for good. But first I had to prove my worth.

Dr Gomarus reappeared before us, facing us like an examining magistrate.

'Can either of you two boys read or write?'

Pyotr and I both shook our heads, and Mrs Pafnutkin, detecting criticism, worked her shoulders beneath her shawl as if against the cold.

'No call for readers and writers in a wash-house, your excellency,' she sniffed.

'What about numbers? What is seventeen add eight?'

I knew Pyotr was better at numbers than me (he and his friends played cards) but faced with a simple question, all he did was colour up even more. '*Sir—twenty-five,*' I said breathlessly.

'Good . . . And forty-two take away nine?'

'Thirty-three, sir,' I answered.

Dr Gomarus nodded sagely and I felt his interest shift more my way. When he spoke next, it was as if Pyotr wasn't there.

'How about a problem . . . ? If a farmer takes twelve hens to market and sells them for four draculs each, how—'

'*Four draculs,*' I said in disbelief. 'Begging your pardon, sir; why, he should ask at least seven.'

'The boy's not daft there, your excellency,' agreed Mrs Pafnutkin. 'He's being robbed. Four draculs is daylight robbery.'

'There might have been something wrong with them,' volunteered the tall toothy lad from the ironing room. 'Perhaps they were sick.'

'Then he had no business selling them,' declared Mrs Pafnutkin seething in self-righteous anger. 'It's the bad food we eat that makes us ill half the time.'

Other views then followed thick and fast.

'At that price I would buy one.'

'Me too.'

'I would make a stew.'

'But you would roast the giblets?'

'Of course.'

'Yes, and you could always buy some potatoes with the money you've saved.'

'Or turnips.'

'Unless you had them already, then you could buy some bread . . .'

And so it went on until a bewildered Dr Gomarus threw up his hands in surrender.

'Please—*enough*. I'll take the boy!'

We walked along Cigarette Factory Road together—me and my new master—a wary distance between us. A silence hanging in the air. In

Dr Gomarus's pocket a grubby piece of paper signing over my life to him. Like a slave—but a willing one. I winced.

'What's wrong?'

'These boots, sir. They pinch.'

I had left the orphanage with only the rags I stood up in, plus an old workman's jacket and a pair of ex-army boots, for which Mrs Pafnutkin had shamelessly held out her hand and requested another six draculs.

The boot leather, so old, had whitened and hardened solid. It refused to bend.

'You did not complain earlier when you tried the boots on.'

'Begging your pardon, sir, trying them on is one thing, walking in them is another. But thank you. Thank you for the boots . . . sir.'

'Nonsense. Everybody needs boots in the snow.'

We drifted back into silence, me darting glances at Dr Gomarus, still trying to get the measure of him. Just as I was beginning to regret my rashness for ever wanting to escape the harsh dull safety of the orphanage, I heard him speak.

'Boy . . . *Yanis*—'

'Yes, sir?' I spoke eagerly.

'An unusual name that, is it Turktumish or Slavaskian?'

'I don't think either, sir. Mrs Pafnutkin named me after a cat she had a particular fondness for at the time.'

'And was she *particularly* fond of *you*?'

'I shouldn't think so . . . sir.'

'Extraordinary how illogical people can be. What about your parents?'

I shrugged. 'I was found on Mrs Pafnutkin's doorstep, in a cardboard box, sir. She said I was wrapped in a yellow blanket. I suppose that's why yellow has always been my favourite colour.'

'Why? Because of some unremembered sentimental attachment?'

'I really don't know, sir. It's just my lucky colour—that's all.'

'*Humph*. Whatever luck is. Besides, couldn't it be argued that yellow is just as much your *un*lucky colour? After all, it was the colour you were clothed in when you were abandoned to a life in which you were called after a cat and worked like a dog.'

His pink lenses turned to me for a response and he was smiling at his own clever wordplay, but I didn't reply. I didn't dare to. It seemed silly to say I liked yellow because it was the colour of the sun, and summer, and being warm. He seemed to find fault in everything I said. He knew I wasn't clever like he was, and this was just everyday chatter that was not supposed to have any great meaning at all.

18

Now how I wished it had been Pyotr he had chosen. How I wished I could blush and stammer as expertly as he could. Suddenly these things seemed like brilliant devices cunningly used by Pyotr to escape the doctor's clutches.

We walked in silence for the rest of the way.

'Here we are.'

I looked up to see a well-kept lodging-house in the square facing the great domed cathedral of the Holy Blood of Jesus.

'Wait here.'

The doctor sprang lightly up the steps and pulled the bell-pull. A moment later a tall, sharp-featured woman in a purple turban opened the door. Without saying a word, she folded her arms, her eyes travelling straight past Dr Gomarus and fixing themselves critically on me. So intense was her stare that I began to shuffle awkwardly in my stiff army boots.

'Is that him? The new one?'

Dr Gomarus nodded.

'Well, doctor, didn't I tell you that if you go fishing for orphans you must throw the small ones back?'

'I'm afraid, Mrs Tiverzin, I made do from a bad lot.'

'Well, get him in and quickly, before the neighbours notice and think I am setting up home for strays and beggars. *Quickly—quickly*. Bring him straight through to the kitchen; everything has been made ready.'

I did not like the sound of this. What did she mean 'made ready'? Despite my reluctant foot-steps, Dr Gomarus had pushed me through the doorway, into the hall, my mind turning over every disagreeable possibility as to what it might be. However nothing—*nothing*—prepared me for the full horror of the thing set up and waiting for me in the middle of the kitchen floor. Seeing it—a tin bath full of clean, steaming water—I took a step backwards in shock, but the doors were shut. I was trapped.

As if to torment me further, Mrs Tiverzin made an airy gesture in the direction of the range; on it what must have been every pan she owned stood brimming with water.

'Plenty more hot to come,' she said gleefully, rolling up her sleeves. 'Now, come on, lad, off with these rags.'

Appearing to lose interest in me, Dr Gomarus sat down on the kitchen table, one foot raised on a chair, loosening the coils of his scarf from around his neck.

'You best do what Mrs Tiverzin says. She hates dirt as much as your Mrs Pafnutkin seems to find virtue in it.'

'But . . .' I wanted to say that washing was what you did to clothes—other people's clothes—that soap was for collars and cuffs, not necks and hair. Besides, taking off your clothes more than once a year was indecent, especially in front of others.

'Come on, I'm waiting!' Grabbing me, Mrs Tiverzin began attacking my buttons. 'Really, boy, you've nothing I haven't seen before. Three husbands have come through that door, and let me tell you, they were carried out a darn sight cleaner than they came in.'

'Perhaps he has cat's blood in him, Mrs Tiverzin. Perhaps he is afraid of water.'

'Then he should have a cat's sense not to get dirty in the first place.'

Mrs Tiverzin's no-nonsense efficiency left me too weak to struggle.

'Please, ma'am, I don't want a bath,' I whispered. 'Bathing weakens you and makes you sick.'

'That so?' said Mrs Tiverzin. 'Then we'll carve it on your gravestone. "The poor child died of soap and water." *Now keep still.*'

I had become a challenge to her, for although I put up no resistance, my clothes did, for every buttonhole was clogged with dirt, and like all Mrs Pafnutkin's orphans, I had been sewn into my rags, with layers of newspapers in-between for extra warmth. In the end none of this proved a defence against Mrs Tiverzin. She attacked the stitches with a knife, then tore open my shirt. A bundle of newspapers fell to the floor along with such a sprinkling of dirt that Mrs Tiverzin declared it was like a fall of soot down an unswept chimney.

Dr Gomarus stooped to pick up one of the grubby sheets.

'Nearly eight months out of date,' he said, eyebrows arching in astonishment. Then with a dramatic flourish he read out the main headline. *'Royalist forces close in on Nikolay Kolchak.'*

Hearing this, I couldn't help myself, I let out a small cry of surprise.

'What? What is it, boy?'

Dr Gomarus peered at me as if I were an unusual bug that had just landed on his wrist.

'Sir, that name, sir.'

'Nikolay Kolchak? Well, what of it?'

'Nothing, sir . . . only Mrs Pafnutkin used to tell us tales about him. She said he is the most godless man ever to walk the earth, and that if you ever met him and his company of half-demons, it would be better for you if you threw yourself on your dagger than suffer at their hands. Better still if you fell dead of shock, or so Mrs Pafnutkin used to say. And if ever the little ones were being heavy on the soap, she'd make them cry by telling them how Nikolay Kolchak punished such wasters by nailing their fingers to a tree.'

'Did she? Well, there's a warning for you, Mrs Teverzin. Go easy with that bar of yours.'

Mrs Teverzin grinned and rippled her fingers at him. 'I'm prepared to take my chances, doctor. Oh, but the rubbish they fill a child's head with these days, it must scare them half to death.'

'But it's true,' I protested. 'Nikolay Kolchak is the Tsar's greatest enemy.'

Dr Gomarus leaned back, cupping his knee with his hands and half closing his eyes.

'Or the Tsar is Nikolay Kolchak's greatest enemy.'

I felt Mrs Tiverzin stiffen. She shot the doctor a sharp look. 'Now, doctor, there's no call for loose talk like that in *this* house. As for you, young man, you've got nothing to fear. This Nikolay Kolchak— black-hearted he may be but he's just a man like any other: he has arms and legs and a head—'

'Begging your pardon, ma'am, so has the Devil.'

Dr Gomarus snorted loudly then disguised his laughter with a spluttering cough. Mrs Tiverzin, saying no more, pulled a tight mouth and made little sniffing noises as her blade sliced through the last few stitches.

My rags peeled away from me with ridiculous ease, forming a heap upon the floor.

Embarrassed, I covered myself with my hands, at the same time gazing down at my own body with a degree of curiosity. My chest and slightly swollen belly resembled white chicken flesh streaked with dirt, while my hands and feet (and a patch just below my throat) were a more robust colour—ruddy and black with muck.

'Into the water, my lad,' ordered Mrs Tiverzin pointing.

As I climbed into the bath, I gave a violent shudder. The heat seemed to cook my skin. Sitting down, I drew up my knees to my chin pro-tectively, noticing a scab on one knee the size of a five dracul coin.

But if I had hoped to enjoy a few leisurely moments picking it before getting out again, I had clearly not understood Mrs Tiverzin's mean-ing of 'a proper bath', and the next moment she advanced on me, armed with soap and scrubbing-brush and began her work. And what terrible work it was—I howled and begged for mercy. Surely if keeping clean causes a person this much pain, it can't be right or good for him? And I said so—or at least I tried to say so . . .

To Dr Gomarus I was entertainment—a comic turn. He chuckled to himself as he skinned an apple with his penknife in one unbroken peeling. I felt the same was being done to me. My skin stung. And Mrs Tiverzin, fine torturer that she was, said, 'Oh, be quiet, you big baby. If you didn't go on so, you wouldn't swallow so much water.'

But seeing how brown the water had turned gave me a new reason to howl.

'Dr Gomarus! Dr Gomarus! Look! I'm melting.'

Mrs Tiverzin tutted. 'Melting indeed. It's only the years of filth being driven out.' And to Dr Gomarus she said, 'Dear me, doctor, you may find yourself with a boy half the size of the one you started out with.'

'Ah yes.' He beamed agreeably. 'They do say delicates shrink in the wash.'

My ordeal only ended when Mrs Tiverzin finally ran out of parts of me to scrub. (I'm sure she wished I was a great deal bigger.)

'There, my lad,' she pronounced like a booming prophetess, when done. 'There's a lesson to be learned in the benefits of soap and a tub of hot clean water.'

If there was, I think I was beginning to learn it. For soon the stinging sensation on my skin gave way to a warm tingling glow, and my body, no longer that goose-pimply chicken-skin white, was smooth cherry-blossom pink. I had changed colour like a winter fox, but it felt to me as if my whole body was new. The feeling made me light-headed. I wondered if this was what it was to be drunk.

I stood gathered up in a fluffy towel, examining my arms, while Mrs Tiverzin prodded deep into my ears with a twisted-up corner of a rag.

'It's a regular wax mine in here,' she complained to Dr Gomarus. 'Find some wicks, doctor, and we could make our fortune selling candles.'

When Dr Gomarus didn't reply, I looked up and saw he was no longer sitting on the table. Twisting away from Mrs Tiverzin, I saw that he was kneeling down at the range, pushing the last of my clothes into the fire.

Even my new coat and boots!

'*My clothes,*' I gasped. 'What are you doing? Am I expected to go round with nothing on?'

'It would be rather draughty,' agreed Dr Gomarus standing up and dusting his hands. Then from under the table he produced a box full of good-quality second-hand clothes.

Mrs Tiverzin laid her hand on my shoulder.

'With a nip here and a tuck there, we could make something half decent out of you—and if not, it won't be from want of trying.'

And true to her word, she set about me with a renewed vigour, making me try on now this shirt, now that, now this waistcoat, now that, thoughtfully pressing her chin with her thumb and turning me around to view me from every angle.

'Now try these trousers with that jacket . . .'

I never once refused. It seemed mean to complain when I was getting a brand-new wardrobe and all that was being asked of me was a little patience. Afterwards I closed my eyes and lightly ran my fingertips over collars and cuffs, testing myself on the materials and hardly believing they belonged to me.

Mrs Tiverzin's own busy fingers were jerkily tying the strings of her apron.

'That's your outsides dealt with, now what about your insides? Are you hungry, Yanis?'

'Perhaps . . . maybe a little.'

'Well, get yourself sat down with the good doctor and I'll get you something to eat.'

Meekly I edged myself into a chair and shortly afterwards a plate was thrust in front of me.

I stared down at it.

'You can eat it, you know,' said Mrs Tiverzin. 'It's not an exhibit at a museum—it's not a work of art.'

Oh, but it was. A masterpiece on clean white china. My mouth filled with saliva at the sight of it . . . Cold sausage, pickled cabbage, sourdough bread thickly spread with fresh butter, and a pickled egg.

Overwhelmed, I bowed my head and pushed my hands deeper into my lap.

Taking this as criticism, Mrs Tiverzin sniffed and said, 'No one usually complains about my food, do they, doctor? Folk don't usually act as if I'm trying to poison them.'

I said nothing, even though it made me look stupid or ungrateful, for how could I make her understand that at the orphanage we lived on an unchanging diet of buckwheat gruel, rye bread, and pork fat, only getting proper meat at Christmas and Easter. Then—at those times— some stringy unidentifiable part of a stewed rabbit was slopped up to us as a treat. We ate only to stop the pains in our bellies from getting worse; we ate because the only other choice was starving.

I could see Dr Gomarus watching me closely and this made me nervous and clumsy as I began to eat, using my fingers instead of the fork Mrs Tiverzin had provided.

The pickled cabbage first—*sharp*—*vinegary*. Then a tiny morsel of bread, holding it before my face and smiling because the butter was so yellow—I trapped it in my mouth for many seconds before starting to chew. The egg was so perfect I couldn't bear to break it, but when I did, there was that same glorious yellow again, hidden inside. Then the sausage—the best till last. Slowly I raised it to my mouth, slowly my teeth bit into it—spicy hot and good.

My mind was so flooded with flavours and sensations that I was hardly aware of anything else. I did not know what my other hand was doing until Dr Gomarus hauled it out of my pocket and made it return the remaining portion of sausage to the plate.

'No, Yanis, you don't have to hoard your food—I promise while you're with me you will not know hunger.'

Quite to my surprise, I suddenly and violently burst into tears, and I sobbed and sobbed until I shook.

The doctor and Mrs Tiverzin showed me other little kindnesses in a hundred different ways, for which I had no means of paying them back except to thank them over and over until the words turned stale in my mouth. Mrs Tiverzin was particularly diligent on my behalf, spending several hours hunched over a candle with her half-moon spectacles on the tip of her nose, and a needle and thread in her hand, altering my new clothes. And at bedtime, I found that a place had been made ready for me at the bottom of the wardrobe in Dr Gomarus's room. It had been cleaned out and lined with blankets and pillows, none of which was torn or stained. I thought it the best bed in the world, and Dr Gomarus's bedroom the best room, with nothing in it that was worn or broken. Besides the wardrobe, it had a chair, and a chest of drawers, and a desk to write at, while Dr Gomarus's own bed was made of twisted brass tubes. Not an object there was out of place, and the room smelt of beeswax and was lit by a candle *and* an oil-lamp; yet perhaps the greatest extravagance of all was the fire in the grate.

Standing warming myself before the flames, I thought of my old companions shivering beneath their sacks in the attic of the orphanage and— may God forgive me—it gave me a strange kind of pleasure knowing I was here and they weren't.

'Here—you'll need this.'

Dr Gomarus flung a nightshirt at me and sat down at the desk to finish a letter. As I fumbled with unfamiliar buttons, trying not to disturb him, I listened to the comforting sounds of coals set- tling and the scratch of Dr Gomarus's nib upon paper. I watched him write, noticing how low he bent his head to read his words; so low in fact that

I grew worried in case he set his hair ablaze with the candle.

'Oh . . . it's no use . . . This confounded light . . .'

Dr Gomarus gave up and threw down his pen. Taking off his pink spectacles, he massaged his eyes with his thumbs. I finished folding up my clothes and, in my socks and nightshirt, knelt down by my bed, head bowed, hands together, my voice a discreet murmur.

'God bless the Tsar,
Keep him strong and in health.
God bless the Tsarina,
May she extend to us her love and kindness.
God bless the little Tsarevich,
And his sisters the imperial princesses.
God watch over our government,
And keep us safe from our enemies.
God bless me,
And help me to serve my country in every way
   I can.

Amen.'

'So you believe in all that, do you?'

'Sir?' I stood up to face him.

'Prayer. You really believe it makes a difference?' I could hear the smile in his voice.

'Of course, sir. At the orphanage, we prayed every night. Mrs Pafnutkin said if we didn't pray, the Devil would send imps in the form of fleas to nip us as we slept. She said a flea would bite us for every evil deed and thought we'd had that day.'

Dr Gomarus snorted contemptuously.

'Don't you believe it, boy. A flea is no more part of the supernatural world than you or I; its actions, like ours, governed by needs and instincts. Why, I daresay a flea would bite the body of the Holy Mother herself if it was on the look-out for a meal of warm blood. Have you heard of the Englishman Sir Ulric Burton . . . ? No, I suppose you won't have. Well, in his book *Angels Without Wings* he makes an excellent case for mankind evolving from bears and not descending from Adam and Eve as we've been told to accept on blind faith. In my view he proves his theory most conclusively.'

Shocked by his words, I scrambled beneath my blankets. I hoped the doctor was not a heathen. Or worse. After all, didn't Nikolay Kolchak stable his horses in churches and use the holy relics as targets?

He watched me for a moment or two, then said, 'Was Mrs Pafnutkin a deeply religious woman, would you say?'

'I don't think so, sir.'

'So why did she make you pray so earnestly?'

'I think it was in case a man came from the Town Hall and asked about our—now, what did she call it?—*moral welfare*. That's it—*moral welfare.*'

Dr Gomarus's smile broadened.

'Ah, so your prayers weren't directed at God in his everlasting heaven, but at some downtrodden little pen-pusher tucked away in a dismal back room in a government office?'

Highly amused by this, he suddenly threw back his head and laughed. When he saw I was not laughing with him, however, he had the decency to stop.

'Don't mind me, boy,' he said softly. 'I am a man of science, I need proof in all things. But it doesn't mean I'm not a good man.'

'I know that, sir. You have been kinder to me than all the saints in Heaven.'

'Hmm. I shall take that as a compliment.' Then he laughed again, saying, 'Do you snore, Yanis?'

'Me, sir? I don't know, sir. I'll try not to.'

'Good lad.'

Blowing out the candle, Dr Gomarus crossed over and sat on the edge of his bed, tugging off his boots. For his own modesty's sake he went behind a screen to undress. I lay in my bed, hands beneath my head, contented, my eyes moving around the room to cherish every single detail again. It seemed to me now that there were some things I hadn't noticed well enough the first

33

time—the black and white print above the fire-place being one of them.

I studied it now.

It showed a sweeping stairway at some grand building—a palace, no doubt. Gathered there upon it was a great throng of generals and ladies, and despite the crush, everyone had stepped back to allow passage for the imperial family. The grandest of all families stood at the head of the stairs, pausing a moment to be admired. Leading it as he led everything was Tsar Vladmir, his chest covered in ribbons and medals, and a boar-crested helmet clamped firmly beneath his arm. Slightly behind him was his beautiful Austrian wife, the Tsarina; then came their sickly twin daughters, dressed identically, huge floppy bows in their hair. And last of all in the group, the Tsarevich, a small boy in a sailor suit, gripping the hand of his stern-faced nanny, and looking as lost as I—Yanis the ragamuffin—was, now that all my familiar sights and routines had been swept away.

I felt a strange twinge inside and smiled, wondering if it was happiness, the feeling as rare to me as clean sheets next to my skin.

The smile was still on my face when Dr Gomarus finally stepped out from behind the screen, wearing a patched and buttonless nightshirt.

He hurriedly slipped into bed as if embarrassed to be seen in it, the bedsprings creaking.

'Goodnight, Yanis.'

'Goodnight, sir.'

Dr Gomarus leant across and turned off the oil-lamps.

I kept my eyes open.

The glow of the fire made even the darkness friendly.

Early the next morning I was awoken by a scratching at the door. I opened my eyes to cold, dead darkness; Dr Gomarus moaned and turned in his bed, the bedsprings marking his movement.

'Dr Gomarus?'

The door opened just wide enough to admit Mrs Tiverzin's turbaned head. In one hand she held a candle, its flame protected by her other hand, casting the shadow of her fingers upon the wall.

Her voice, when she spoke, was as soft as the candle-light.

'It's time to get up, Dr Gomarus. Shall I build up the fire for you?'

'No . . . no, thank you, Mrs Tiverzin. We shall be gone long before any benefit might be gained from it.'

'As you please.'

The door closed.

Dr Gomarus got out of bed and I heard him fumble about in the darkness until a match was struck and the candle lighted. He found his cut-throat razor and prepared to shave, although, curiously, he meant to do so in cold water and without a mirror. Nor, when the time came, did he shave with any great care, feeling for whiskers with his finger-tips. I heard the scrape of bristles and saw that the soap he flicked from his blade was spotted with blood.

When done, he put away the basin of scummy water on a lower ledge of the iron washstand and, taking up a clean basin, filled it with water from a jug. He gasped as he washed his face, neck, and arms—finishing by reaching under his nightshirt to wash his chest—the room cold enough to show each gasp as a short-lived cloud. Turning to me, I saw how the little drips along his chin sparkled like diamonds. And I thought how much older he looked with his hair unkempt, and with his eyes screwed-up and unfocused.

'Come on, Yanis, time for you to stir yourself too.'

I crawled out of the wardrobe not sure what I had to do, so I copied the doctor and washed myself at the same washstand, doing the minimum I could with the least amount of water.

Then Dr Gomarus reappeared dressed from behind the screen. To me, taking clothes off and putting them back on again remained something of a novelty, but again following his example I dressed myself quickly, shivering at the cold touch of my shirt upon my back. As I did up my buttons, I watched Dr Gomarus take a small leather bag from under the bed and begin to fill it with his things.

'You can put your stuff in here too,' he told me. 'There's plenty of room. I sent on most of my luggage and equipment yesterday.'

'Would that be equipment used in your work, sir?'

'It would.'

'You haven't told me yet, sir, what it is you do.'

'No—I haven't.'

And he finished packing in silence.

In the kitchen, Mrs Tiverzin was again on the verge of tears. She acted as if she was losing her favourite son and not a paying lodger.

'You haven't time for breakfast, doctor, so I've packed you a few rations. Mind you eat them, you hear?' She turned to me. 'You make sure he eats properly, boy, and doesn't just nibble on a few crumbs like a sparrow. I know what he's like. Once he gets into his work he doesn't know what day it is.'

I promised to do my best, and in a wild burst of gratitude, Mrs Tiverzin swept down on me and hotly kissed both my cheeks. Then she kissed Dr Gomarus who smiled sheepishly in his over-large coat like a bewildered child. She insisted on kissing us again at the front door; across the way the darkened shape of the cathedral like a sleeping giant. Above, the frosty morning stars.

'You be careful on these frozen streets. Watch out you don't slip and break a leg. *Oh*, and God speed your journey—although the Almighty alone knows why you should want to turn your back on civilization and go gallivanting off to the back of beyond.'

'You must ask Him when you see Him.'

'*Doctor*—such sacrilege!'

'Goodbye, Mrs Tiverzin.'

'Goodbye—goodbye to you both. You take care of him, boy. Remember: regular meals and fewer late nights.'

With a final wave we set off, carrying the leather bag between us, a handle apiece, and heading towards the river. Perhaps mindful of Mrs Tiverzin's warning, we walked down the middle of the road where servants had scattered last night's ashes for the coal and milk wagons. Ahead, a cold colourless light was creeping up the sky like ice on a windowpane.

The city's silence made us silent—for the moment neither of us wanting to waste warmth on words. Besides, from the nose down, Dr Gomarus's face was muffled in a scarf, his breath coming through it like steam from a leaky piston. For all anyone knew, he might have been a bandit, his shapeless fur hat pulled down to his eyes.

Apart from ourselves the ice-bound streets were deserted; we didn't meet another soul until we reached the big paper mill on Archangel Street. There the shift was changing, streams of grey workers pouring out of the gateway, the early morning shift hurrying to clock on. I decided now was the time to ask the doctor a question I wanted to know the answer to, almost as badly as I wanted to know his line of business. And perhaps this time he would give me a proper reply.

'Sir,' I began, 'where are we going?'

He pulled down his scarf just enough to uncover his mouth.

'You know perfectly well where. To board our ship.'

'Yes, sir, of course to board our ship. But where is the ship going?'

His lips parted.

'—And please don't say *east*, I know that already. Mrs Tiverzin seemed to know, she said it was *the back of beyond*.'

'For Mrs Tiverzin the shops are the back of beyond.'

'Oh, *sir*.'

He sighed.

'Very well, since you press me so hard for a name, I shall give you one. *Osva*. There, are you happy? Is your curiosity sufficiently satisfied?'

I wasn't sure. *Osva*. I said the name to myself, then again more solemnly. The doctor had spoken it as if it should mean something, but to me it meant nothing at all.

He turned to me with a superior expression on his face.

'You see, you are no wiser for knowing, are you, boy?'

I shook my head.

'No, sir. Not really.'

'Which is just what I thought.'

And with that he pulled up his scarf to show the matter was now closed. But if he thought I was content with this, he was wrong. For what exactly had he told me? Nothing. Just *Osva*. But what was this Osva? Was it a city? Was it a district? And why was he being so mysterious about it?

My brow wrinkled in thought as we turned into a narrow alley that ran past the backs of the Jewish merchants' houses, down the hill towards the docks: me keeping pace with the doctor, the bag between us. So in step, in fact, that when the doctor suddenly stopped, the handle was almost wrenched from my grasp. I saw him staring ahead and turned to see what was troubling him.

By rights it should have been a gang of armed ruffians, to judge by his reaction. But it wasn't. All there was, was a slogan hastily daubed in red paint, the letters large and uneven, and the paint still fresh enough to be dribbling down the wall.

'What is it?' I asked, instinctively whispering. 'What does it say?'

Trance-like, Dr Gomarus pulled down his scarf until his throat was completely uncovered.

'*Kill the traitor. Kill the Tsar.*' His eyes widened in horror. He glanced behind. 'Good God in Heaven, did I just say that aloud?'

'Kill the Tsar? But, sir, who would want to do such a wicked thing?'

The answer hit me even as I spoke the question. Now it was my turn to glance behind.

'Nikolay Kolchak?'

'Yanis, don't be so idiotic.' Dr Gomarus rounded on me almost angrily. 'That Pafnutkin creature at the orphanage has told so many half-truths and fairytales that you accept them without question. Do you really believe Nikolay Kolchak is a bogey-man who comes for little children in the night? And do you honestly think he is the only one with a grudge against the Tsar? Well, do you? Let me tell you straight, boy, that in some parts of the country there's practically a civil war raging, with revolutionaries and royalists at each other's throats. And where there isn't outright fighting, there are strikes and lockouts and acts of arson and sabotage. It's those who demand change against those determined to keep the old order at any price, with the Tsar at its head. It's black against white; it's fire against water. It's hostages and exe-cutions and assassinations. And if you do not choose one side or the other, then, my lad, you'd better make sure you aren't caught up in the crossfire. Come on—*hurry*. We mustn't be dis-covered here.'

Swept up by the doctor's urgency, I raced alongside him down the icy cobbles. The doctor's words and the way he had spoken frightened me, without my fully understanding why. After all *we* had done nothing wrong—I could barely scratch out my own name, let alone cover a wall in dirty threats against our beloved father, the Tsar (long may he reign over us).

For once I was happy to be stupid. Then, catching sight of a splash of red paint in the snow, my mouth grew so dry that my breath rattled in my throat.

We ran on, trying to escape the alley, like rats trying to escape a trap, and still it went on sloping down to the river in endless twists, a blind high wall on either side, topped with spikes, with bolted gates and doors leading to darkened yards, and now and again a boarded-up stable or shuttered workshop. Guard-dogs were alert to us and flew into a frenzy at the sound of our approach.

'Come on, Yanis,' urged the doctor, but my boots kept slithering and losing their grip.

Then something happened.

From out of the darkness a figure appeared, as unaware of us as we were of him until we slammed into each other. To stop myself falling backwards, my hands flew up and caught the lapels of his distinctive blue coat, feeling a rich blend of wool and cashmere. Holding on to him, keeping myself steady, the stranger and I found ourselves gazing into each other's astonished face. He was, I saw, a young man with a crooked nose, and yet it was his eyes I noticed most of all, they almost filled my sight, so wide were they with cold stark terror. Then roughly he shook me off, thrust something into Dr Gomarus's free hand, and scrambled away up the hill.

All this happened in the space of a few breathless moments. When the stranger had gone, the doctor and I stared stupidly at what he had given us. A half-empty pot of red paint and a paint-sodden brush. Dr Gomarus was horrified. With a shuddering cry he threw the pot away as if it were cursed, as perhaps it was. For out of the darkness, from the direction the young man had appeared, came the sound of hooves galloping towards us.

'The doorway over there!' yelped Dr Gomarus.

It was the nearest we could find to a hiding place, the door it led to set back a pace or two from the alley. I arrived there first, only to be crushed against the heavy door by Dr Gomarus. The door handle dug into my back and the bag into my side; and as painfully cramped as I was, I knew that Dr Gomarus was using his body to shield me.

We had hidden just in time. A moment later three horsemen arrived on the scene and reined up by the discarded paint pot. Each rider, dressed in black, held his sabre military style, the blade curving over his shoulder. Wordlessly they gazed down at the paint. The furthest rider, his lip misshapen by a livid scar, raised an eyebrow knowingly; beside him his bearded companion sat back in the saddle with a satisfied sigh. They turned to the third of their company who—still without a single word exchanged between them— slowly resheathed his sword and dismounted.

Hunkering down by the pot, he took out a box of matches and struck several at once on the toe of his boot. The matches fizzled and flared, seeming to drive back every shadow, leaving the doctor and me so hopelessly revealed that, with a simple glance to the side, any one of the three men would have spotted us. But then the flame steadied, small and weak, and the shadows came racing back. This might have made me more glad had I been able to move. Crushed against the door, I began to feel sick: it was just as well that my stomach was empty.

Managing to keep my queasiness under control, I concentrated on what was happening in the alley before me. There I saw the scarred one and bearded one talking together in an undertone, while the crouching one held out his match-light at arm's length to survey the alley as it rose up the hill. I watched him closely. The man was a complete stranger to me. I didn't know his name. But there was something about him I *did* know and that was what he was. I knew what all three of them were. They were members of the Tsar's secret police.

Just admitting that made my skin go cold, for at the orphanage we had feared the secret police almost as much as we had feared revolutionaries. And it was easy to see why. Served by a network of spies and informants, and with a sinister fondness for dark clothing, they were in charge of security and responsible for hunting down enemies of the Tsar. Mrs Pafnutkin told us that they listened at doors and windows and would cut off our tongues with their sabres if ever we spoke badly of the royal family. But then the secret police were just about everywhere and everyone knew who they were. Their headquarters was the big granite building on the corner of Commerce Street with an unmarked door at the side. That was well known too, so well known that some crossed the road to avoid it, while others preferred not to walk in its shadow. In fact the only really secret thing about the secret police was the way in which they worked; that and what became of the poor devils they took away.

But wait. My being afraid of them didn't make sense. Wasn't I as loyal to the Tsar as any of his subjects? Didn't I pray for him and his family every night? Surely those men would see that. Just as they would see that the paint had nothing to do with the good doctor and me, and our hiding ourselves away, well, it was nothing more than a misunderstanding. They knew who the real enemy was. All I had to do was cry out 'Long live the Tsar' and everything would be fine.

In my nervousness I must have muttered aloud something of my intentions, making Dr Gomarus aware, for the instant I tried to fill my lungs, he pushed back with such force that a squeak became impossible, let alone a patriotic roar.

When I looked again, I saw that the secret policeman had remounted, a spent match drooping from the corner of his mouth.

'He won't get far,' he mumbled. 'The fool hasn't the sense to realize there's paint on the sole of his shoe. He's laying us a trail to follow wherever he runs.'

The scarred one sucked spit through his teeth and spat on the ground; the bearded one gave a bored grunt as if such an easy chase wasn't worth the effort. Then, edging their horses daintily around the pool of paint, they galloped off in pursuit.

Only when certain they were out of earshot did the doctor release me. He stepped forward primly adjusting his hat and coat, and pushing his spectacles up his nose.

'Never ever try anything like that again, boy,' he said peevishly. 'And just you remember, when we board the *Ursus*, the whole ship will be crawling with secret police and their agents. *Just you remember.'*

He picked up the bag and strode off without waiting; I trotted after him, mortified and thoroughly chastened.

Ten minutes later we reached the docks. They were protected by a high, stone wall. At the goods' entrance, wagons were lining up to be searched; the passenger entrance, further along, was grander and flanked by two soldiers in sentry boxes. Bayonets fixed. Passing under the archway, we found ourselves in a small busy yard that led into a tin shed. We queued at a table.

'Tickets—boarding passes, please.'

Dr Gomarus produced two tickets and handed them to a brisk young woman, who, despite the wood-burning stove at her back, wore a thick coat and knitted hat.

Holding a pen in her gloved hand, she ticked us off on her passenger list.

'Next.'

The orderlies moved people along efficiently and most were directed straight through the embarkation shed and out the other side; we, however, were shown to a roped-off area and to a second table. At it sat two soldiers, with a third slouching behind against a metal column. On the table a cigarette smouldered in an ashtray, an inch of perfect ash at the end.

'You will have your papers ready.'

The first soldier, writing in a ledger, spoke without looking up. I noticed that his hair grew over his ears and that one or two of his tunic buttons were undone. Around his neck was a medallion with a picture of the Tsar on it.

Dr Gomarus searched nervously in an inside pocket, taking out several sheaves of folded paper.

Still without looking up, the first soldier took them, unfolded them, and passed them to his captain who yawned.

'*You are* Dr Gomarus?'

'Yes.'

'And *that is* Goshka Kulich?'

'Yes, indeed, my assistant.'

Dr Gomarus gave me a brief worried glance. As the soldiers put the fear of God into me, I was relieved not to answer for myself; I guessed Goshka Kulich was the one who had gone down with scarlet fever.

'He is *rather* small for fifteen.'

'Yes . . . very small.'

'Perhaps he is a dwarf,' said the soldier leaning against the column and he laughed sourly to himself.

'*Dr Gomarus*, why do you *consider it necessary* to wear such *curious* spectacles?'

'My eyes . . . they're rather weak; the coloured lenses offer some relief against the light.'

'*So*, you are not *trying to hide* behind them?'

'No, I told you—'

'*Please*. Would you mind removing them a moment.'

Dr Gomarus did as he was asked and blinked at the soldiers who studied his features closely.

'Very well, put them back on. You *must be aware*, doctor, that you are travelling to a *restricted area*.'

'Of course. That's why I waited six months for the correct papers—and spent another three months before that hanging about draughty corridors at the Ministry of Loyalty.'

He realized at once he had said the wrong thing. The captain looked up stonily.

'I *sincerely hope* you are not criticizing *our* methods?'

'Oh, no—no—I never meant to imply—'

'Because in these *uncertain times* we can never be *too* careful, *wouldn't* you agree, *doctor*?'

'Most definitely.'

'I am *glad* to hear it.'

'So if everything is in order . . .'

The captain continued to stare at the papers.

'At the ministry they assured me . . . and . . . well, I am on the Tsar's business.'

The captain looked up, this time more mildly.

'Indeed. *The Tsar's business*. Long live the Tsar.'

He spoke automatically and flatly. He returned the papers to the first soldier, who stamped them and folded them and passed them back to Dr Gomarus.

'Move on now . . . oh, and, doctor, *you do* realize you have paint on your coat?'

'What? Paint . . . ? Oh yes, you mean this. *Ha-ha-ha*. It's nothing, nothing. Please don't concern yourself. My boy can fix it. He's good at removing stains. He used to work in a laundry. Well, if that's . . . I mean . . . shall I . . . er . . .'

'Move on,' repeated the captain more firmly.

'Yes. Move on.'

Stepping away, Dr Gomarus eased out a sigh, and taking out his handkerchief, first dabbed the back of his neck then the spots of paint down his front.

'So, I've got to call myself Goshka Kulich from now on, have I?' I said sulkily because my name was the only thing in the world I could truly call my own, and I did not care for the new one.

51

Dr Gomarus gave up on the paint and put his handkerchief away.

'Only if a policeman questions you, otherwise I will say Yanis is my pet name for you—like a cat. There, everything is restored to how it was. Am I forgiven? Mm? Now let's get away from here, I can feel that army fellow still watching us.'

We rejoined the main flow of people. At the back of the shed was another door, positioned by which was a priest in black robes, holding a bundle of birch sticks. As the passengers passed him, he sprinkled them with holy water and blessed their journey—the passengers tipping him a coin in return.

'Reverend father—you missed out my Rodya,' cried a dumpy woman holding up her small boy to him.

The priest's eyes narrowed irritably, then he flicked water into the boy's face. The boy howled in protest and struck back at his mother with his feet.

'Many thanks, reverend father,' she said, ridiculously grateful.

The priest grinned maliciously, revealing that he had no side teeth, and accepted the extra three draculs that the woman insisted on giving him.

After receiving a light sprinkling of holy water ourselves (Dr Gomarus protesting loudly and sarcastically that he already had insurance), we stepped through the door and were out onto the dock. A cold snow-flecked wind blew off the river, and there, directly before us, rose the masts of the ski-ship *Ursus*, the imperial mail ship.

White and gold.

The sight of it, so large and close and magnificent, stopped me dead in my tracks, unable to believe my eyes ... *White and gold*—and such brilliant white and polished gold at that. For someone who was hungry for a different kind of life this was more than I'd ever expected, this was a whole wedding-cake held out to a starving man. And all at once and from out of nowhere a strange wild laugh burst out of me, attracting odd stares from those who were passing by.

'Whatever's the matter?' asked Dr Gomarus sharply.

I rubbed my nose on the back of my hand.

'Nothing ... It's only a cold, sir.'

'Stay close.' He glanced back at the shed. 'Remember what I've told you and try not to draw unwanted attention to yourself.'

To board the *Ursus* there were two gangways, each leading to a different level and class. First class was at the top of the ship, second and third below it. We joined the line for the second class deck. As we waited, I noticed huddles of poorer-looking people gated up like animals in pens, the women in shawls trying to keep their babies warm and the men in quiet groups, smoking.

'Who are all those people?' I asked.

Hearing my question, a rather pompous little red-faced man, in a hat much too small for him, turned and showed his yellow teeth in an ingratiating smile.

'That would be steerage class,' he said. 'They won't let them board till last, and quite right too. Keep them all together then get them out of sight as quickly as possible. You know what they say about the *Ursus*? On first class you have butlers and maids; on second, stewards and waiters; on third, overseers and supervisors; and on steerage, bruisers to break up the fights.'

'How do you know?' asked Dr Gomarus coldly. 'Have you ever travelled on that particular ticket yourself?'

'*Me? Lord no.*' The man laughed at the very idea. 'Be bad for business if my customers found out I cavorted with low life. *Pianos*. That's my line of business. I sell pianos.'

He handed Dr Gomarus his card, for no other reason (it seemed to me) than to show he could afford to have his name grandly done in gold. Dr Gomarus took it without thanks and slipped it into his pocket. I could tell he intended to throw it away at the first opportunity.

'No,' continued the man, 'I deal with only top-notch families. Not *that* sort.' He lowered his voice. 'It's for *that* sort that those damn revolutionaries want to bring down our beloved Tsar. Huh, want to give *them* the vote, would you believe? Look at them. The only thing a rabble like that would vote for is idleness, complete with a steady flow of vodka and sausage—all at someone else's expense, of course. Workshy, the lot of them.'

I turned away from the man, disliking him intensely. I wondered if in reality he might be a secret policeman, one of those Dr Gomarus had warned me about; after all, anyone could say he sold pianos, just as anyone could call himself Goshka Kulich. Worried in case the man was on to my secret, I fixed my gaze upon the huddles of poor people patiently waiting in the cold for their turn to embark. Music had broken out. A troupe of travelling actors had decided to enliven the tedium of waiting. I heard an accordion, then clapping, and all at once there was dancing—a swirl of smiling faces beaming out from beneath hats and scarves.

The shoulders of the pompous little man rose indignantly. 'Any excuse for a shindig,' he said nastily. 'Any excuse ...'

'*Make way—stand clear.*'

Suddenly the dock had a new distraction. Looking across, I saw the smartly dressed line of first class passengers stand aside for two women being escorted to the ship by four policemen. One woman, squat and plainly dressed in black, had a steely, bulldog expression, her thin-lipped mouth turned down. She marched almost in a military way, the watch pinned to her cloak bouncing up and down upon her bosom.

'Gangway. I really must ask you to step aside. *Please*, ladies and gentlemen.'

Her hand gripped the other woman by the elbow, towing her along so she swayed like a reed. She was young and pale, very pale, her brown hair merging into the silver fox fur of her hat; her dark eyes cast down to avoid the many prying stares. And there and then—with just one glance—I thought her . . . I thought her the most beautiful thing I had ever seen in my whole life.

As I followed her and her party's progress, bobbing up on my toes when they briefly disappeared behind the crowds, I saw them come at last to the foot of the gangway. There they halted.

'No need to come aboard,' the bulldog woman told the escorting policemen. 'I'm perfectly capable of taking care of the Countess from here on. I'm sure she'll be as good as gold under my supervision.'

'Only if you're sure, Miss Mirsky.'

'Of course I'm sure. Off you go. You must have far more important things to do than follow us two women around.'

The policemen saluted and stepped back uncertainly. The Countess never once raised her eyes from the ground, nor did Miss Mirsky relinquish her grip. I watched as she led the Countess unprotesting up the gangway. I watched as they boarded the great white and gold ship.

A steward showed us to our cabin; Dr Gomarus was fretful.

'Did all my luggage arrive safely? There were no problems? Nothing I should be made aware of?'

The steward smiled indulgently. 'I daresay everything is in hand, sir; not much goes wrong aboard the *Ursus* these days. The rest of the world may be coming apart at the seams, but you can count on the *Ursus* running smoothly . . . Here we are, sir, this is your cabin. Fourteen B.'

He used a key on a chain to let us in. The cabin was panelled and had one porthole in the door and another in the wall beside it. Two curtained bunks were built into the opposite wall; the upper reached by a ladder. I hoped this would be mine.

The steward removed a second key from his chain and placed it on a chest of drawers. 'If that will be all, sir?'

'Yes—yes. That will be all.'

The steward bowed stiffly then left, staring at the invisible tip in his palm.

'I think he wanted you to give him some money.'

Dr Gomarus was not listening to me, however, but had knelt down beside a collection of boxes, every one of which was beautifully made in a rich, dark wood, with brass hinges and handles. The one exception was an old pine trunk with what I supposed was the doctor's name stencilled upon it. As he did not bother much with this, I guessed it contained his clothes.

'I hope nothing has been damaged. You know how it is with these fellows. You tell them things are fragile and they say "yes", but as soon as your back is turned they throw them about in such a shameless manner . . . I shan't rest until I've checked that everything is in order.'

'I'll help you, shall I?'

'No—no. You won't know what anything is, you'll only get in the way. Tell you what, you go outside and amuse yourself on deck a while—we'll be setting sail soon. I'll call you when I want you.'

I was not going to argue with him (far from it), and before the doctor changed his mind, I slipped away and happily lost myself in the excited crowds on deck. The passengers had all boarded by now and the gangways were being wheeled back.

'Excuse me. Sorry. Excuse me.'

By pushing and sidestepping and making best use of my size, I managed to make it to the front rail for a clear view of our departure.

Below us, I saw that four teams of men had assembled out on the frozen river, each team lined up and waiting. They were a gaunt sorry lot, each man with sacking over his shoulder for protective padding, and heavy spiked boots to grip the ice; and amongst the buzz of the crowd, I heard someone say that these men were convicts sent to the port to serve out their sentences of hard labour. This was why they were watched over and supervised by mounted police. The river was a cruelly exposed place—every living creature on it subdued by the relentless cold; the horses lowering their heads and flattening their ears against the icy spindrift, which threatened to obliterate them all.

At a command too far off for me to hear, each team of convicts wearily took up a rope from the *Ursus*, placed it upon their padded shoulders and waited. When the wind dropped sufficiently, a new command rang out—half bellowed, half in song.

'Two—three—*heave*, little brothers. *Heave*, little brothers. *Heave*, little brothers . . .'

And the teams heaved, and with each heave the ropes creaked and the men's faces twisted up as if in pain. Under me I felt the ski-ship inch away from the dock, I felt it slide on its great iron runners, over the ice towards the middle of the frozen river.

Steam rose off the convicts' backs as I'd seen it rise off carthorses tackling the steep hill in Brewery Street. Then the ropes went slack and with many cries of 'stand well clear!' both police and convicts raced to the side; and my eyes, which had been directed downward at the ice, now lifted to the sky, for the rigging was suddenly alive with sailors fanning out until every spar was occupied, and calling out to each other that they were in position and ready. A moment later the sails unfurled, filling with wind even as they dropped, moving the ship forward even as they filled.

We were under way.

A tremble of excitement went through me, seeing warehouses and canning factories go by at an ever-increasing rate of knots.

Most people lost interest in the view once the city slipped from sight. It was too bitterly cold to linger out on deck, so they drifted away, confidently knowing where and where not they might go on the ship. Soon I was alone, my feet and hands numb, my face almost blistering with cold. But I would not turn away like the others had, even though there was little to see except snow-laden forest coming down to the river's edge, and the occasional gingerbread-style dacha. No, I could stand the nipping cold for as long as I needed, for I knew if I turned away, the magic of the ski-ship would never again be quite the same.

I sniffed, the insides of my nose smarting at the frosty air. At the orphanage, yesterday's washing would have dried frozen and have to be stacked up like sides of meat. Would anyone there stop a moment and wonder where I was? Perhaps I would never be remembered at Mrs Pafnutkin's again. To make the thought more appealing I turned it around and imagined myself the only person left in the whole world. Captain of his ship, swaying with its motion, listening to the hypnotic hiss of the runners—

Then to my intense annoyance a door slid open, making my pretence seem silly and childish.

A red-nosed man in a fur-lined coat came and stood next to me, his fur collar so ludicrously large that it all but hung off his shoulders. He put down a bottle of schnapps.

'Damn fools are serving it nigh on warm,' he muttered by way of a greeting. 'I told them, I said to them, I want schnapps not a cup of tea, thank you very much; and you should see the way they looked at me, like I was the village idiot. So I said, hold on, hand the bottle over—give it to me. A few minutes out here should do the trick, young-fella-m'lad . . .'

I said nothing, didn't even glance his way. *Who cared* about his stupid schnapps? But still the man chattered on aimlessly (now it was the way the Germans and Poles served schnapps), until finally losing patience I turned to go. As I did, I caught sight of a solitary figure on the upper deck. To my astonishment I saw it was the Countess.

The man must have heard me catch my breath, for he turned and in a most obvious manner gawped up at her.

'You have good taste, young fellow . . . But doesn't she make the goosebumps rise just by looking at her? An ice maiden. Ice in her veins instead of blood. *Ha-ha*, if only I might persuade her to hold this bottle a moment or two.'

Managing to swallow back my anger, I said, 'Who is she? What do you know about her?'

He shrugged. 'Only what everyone else on board knows. Some damn fool countess who offended the Tsar and is being sent into exile.'

He was losing interest in the matter even as he spoke, gazing down at the bottle which he gripped protectively between his feet.

'A couple minutes more, I reckon.'

Yet what little he had told me about the Countess had set my mind racing. From the corner of my eye I watched her move to the other side of the ship and stare out across the land. Was she searching for the home she was leaving behind? I wondered. Or was she trying to imagine living her life as a stranger amongst strangers, away from the people and things she knew so well? Suddenly I felt her powerful sadness; it gripped my chest so tightly I could hardly breathe.

The man picked up the bottle and taking a metal tumbler from his pocket, poured out a measure, offering it first to me.

'There you go, young fel—'

I pushed past him.

'Hey, where you going?'

I didn't reply—my eyes fixed on the tiny handkerchief as it fluttered down from the Countess, landing on the deck nearby.

I ran over and picked it up. When I stood up

again, I saw that the Countess was staring down at me with her sad dark eyes.

Again I could hardly breathe.

I ran to the metal stairs and, not caring that the first class quarters were out of bounds to me, sprang up the steps three at a time, cleared the barrier at the top, and ran over to her.

She drew back, startled.

'You dr-dropped . . . this . . . I-I don't—I shouldn't want you t-to l-lose . . . The handkerchief, I mean.'

She smiled gently and took it from me.

'I am most grateful.'

'Not at—*really*—honestly, it was nothing, anyone would—Pardon, Countess?'

She had spoken and I had gone blathering all over her words.

Softly she repeated her question. 'What is your name?'

'Yanis—I mean Goshka. *No*, I mean *Yanis*—'

She smiled.

'Yanis suits you better, I shall call you Yanis—that is, if I may?'

'Of course, Countess. Call me whatever pleases you best.'

Then to my great surprise, she reached out and slowly stroked the line of my jaw with her gloved hand.

'Where are you heading, Yanis?'

'To Osva, Countess.'

'*What?* To the end of the line, like me? Then perhaps we shall meet again in Osva. Perhaps we shall become great friends there. You see, Yanis, I'm all alone in the world at the moment. What I need more than anything else is a friend.'

'A friend?'

She smiled, then I saw the smile freeze on her face.

'*Yanis—your hand.*'

I followed her gaze and saw blood dripping from my palm. I must have caught it on something sharp as I leapt over the barrier, but being so cold I hadn't felt the pain. I felt none now. Embarrassed, I tried to hold my hand out of sight behind my back, hearing the blood drip off my fingers, but the Countess took my arm and gently pulled it back again.

She dabbed the gash with her handkerchief and it was all I could do not to snatch my hand away.

'It looks a lot worse than it is,' she said.

'Truly, Countess, you shouldn't trouble yourself. You'll dirty your gloves.'

'Then I shall wear another pair.'

She looked up and smiled at me.

Hesitantly I smiled back.

'*Countess.*'

With a crash a door slid open and Miss Mirsky appeared, snorting like a bull, the little silver watch bouncing on her bosom.

I sprang back from the Countess as if caught doing her some great harm.

'What's going on here, lady? Who is this boy? And what were you telling him just now? You know you are not permitted to talk to strangers without my consent.'

For the first time I saw the Countess's face flush with anger, but her voice remained calm.

'He is a dear child who was good enough to rescue my handkerchief, Miss Mirsky. Surely it is no crime to give him a few words of kindness in return?'

'*Humph!*'

Clearly Miss Mirsky thought it was.

'It landed on the deck below—' I tried to explain.

Miss Mirsky glared triumphantly.

'The deck below . . . ? Then you should not be up here. This is first class for first class passengers only. Return to your own level before I fetch someone to you. Go on, you wretched child. *Shoo! Shoo!*'

Positioning herself between the Countess and me, Miss Mirsky drove me back towards the stairs, her chest thrust out like a turkey cock.

'Do you hear, boy. *Shoo!*'

It was all very well her saying this, but climbing the barrier was more difficult when I had to think about it. My foot got jammed, Miss Mirsky gave me a hefty shove, and I tumbled backwards, rolling all the way down the stairs.

Lying in a dazed heap at the bottom, I opened my eyes to see Miss Mirsky peering over the rail and grinning nastily.

'Serves you right if that hurt. It would never have happened had you stayed down there in the first place. Now kindly don't bother us again.'

And turning, she reclaimed the Countess and marched her away.

Only when they were gone did I realize that Mr Schnapps was kneeling at my side. This time I accepted the tumbler he held out to me and emptied it in one.

I regretted it immediately.

As I coughed and spluttered and wiped away the tears that streamed from my eyes, Mr Schnapps refilled his tumbler.

He raised it high.

'Here's to gallantry.'

Having found my time out on deck a little too eventful, I decided to return to the doctor, although I still hadn't received any word from him. When I reached our cabin, he met me excitedly at the door.

'Ah, Yanis, the very chap—but what's this? Have you hurt yourself?'

I pushed my hand into my pocket and shook my head. He accepted this without question and quickly forgot he had asked.

'Come in—come see.'

I followed him inside, my eyes, more used to the snow's brilliance, taking a while to adjust. Consequently the cabin seemed small and dark and gloomy. And very hot. My nose began to drip like a thawing tap; I sniffed and wiped it on my sleeve.

The doctor, confident he had my attention, crossed over and stood beaming beside his precious mahogany boxes with their shiny brass hinges and handles; and I saw at once that every box had been opened up—lids and doors thrown back, drawers pulled out—and clearly this had all been done for me.

'Come nearer, you won't wear anything out by looking at it.'

Drawn by my intense curiosity, I went forward and knelt down in front of the biggest box, as respectful of it as of a Christmas crib. But instead of donkeys and wise men, it contained mysterious bottles of coloured liquids, and jars of crystals, and tiny spoons, and silver funnels and delicate glass pipes, and measuring jugs. This told me very little, so I turned to the next box, which housed books and pens and papers, such as any travelling gentleman might own. But the next box contained the parts of some strange disassembled machine whose purpose I couldn't even guess at; and the red velvet-lined box after that took me so much by surprise that I shrank back in horror.

'*Doctor!*'

I turned to him accusingly but he merely smiled at my squeamishness.

'Don't worry, they're each over a hundred years old. From the battlefield at Gorholm. I'm not a grave-robber, if that's what you think. Go ahead, take one out, examine it for yourself. I believe the middle one is General Shevchenko, but he won't mind if you don't salute.'

'I'd rather not, thank you.'

I pursed my lips disapprovingly and respectfully closed the doors on the six human skulls.

Quickly I moved on, yet the next box seemed hardly less sinister to me, for it contained nothing but human eyes, arranged in order of colour, starting at the top left-hand corner with an eye of palest blue and working through each tiny degree of change until the sequence ended with an eye of deepest brown at the bottom right-hand corner.

'Made of glass,' explained Dr Gomarus, 'and very expensive.'

'I expect they were, but what are they for?'

He picked one up and turned it around so that it was 'looking' at me.

'For a man of science, they present an accurate record of the human eye in all its forms. You see, Yanis, I believe the eye is more than just an organ for seeing; I believe if you can know and read the secrets of the eye, you can know a lot about the whole man. And what is true of the eye is equally true of the entire human head, for isn't it shaped by the brain? And isn't the brain the key to us being ourselves? One who knows what to look for might read a living head like a map. You have to understand the clues—the size and shape of a nose or chin, the position of the ears, the fleshiness of a mouth, the formation of the bones in the skull . . .'

This sounded dangerously like wizardcraft to me. But the doctor didn't look like one of those half-mad hermits who made a living out of boiling up herbs in the forest or muttering over chicken entrails, who the desperate go to only as a last resort.

I looked at him with a cool and steady gaze.

'What sort of secrets can be learned from a person's head?'

'Character, behaviour, health, disposition—oh, many things.'

'You really can tell all that from *a person's head*? From its shape and size and how things are, or even by the colour of their eyes?'

Dr Gomarus nodded.

'We all can to a certain extent; for instance, what were your impressions of me when we first met?'

'I thought you looked . . . *umm* . . . a little bit different,' I said, guiltily remembering, 'but underneath I thought you might be kind . . . honest . . . *trustworthy*.'

'*Looked*, you said, *looked*. *Ha-ha*. What part of me were you looking at exactly?'

'Your face I sup—'

'*Precisely. My face*. It is something we all do, albeit clumsily at times. My job, as a scientist, is to give method and precision to all that. It is the reason we are travelling to Osva.'

'We are going to Osva to study heads? Why? And why did you need special permission to go?'

'Because of the prison there. It holds political prisoners—rebels against the Tsar. And we are being given free access to them. It appears my work has come to the attention of some fairly important men with friends in the government. It might be truer to say they were excited by it. In these troubled times they see a great purpose in what I do, and they have set me a challenge. They want me to use my scientific reasoning to identify their enemies.'

'How?'

'If the formation of the head can tell me if a man is likely to be a criminal or mentally unstable, why not a revolutionary? There must be a common factor they all share.'

'You mean they will look alike?'

'No—no, nothing so crude as that. It might be something not noticeable at a glance—such as the angle of the brow above the nose or the configuration of the eyes. I do not know yet, but I mean to find out.'

'When you do, perhaps the Tsar will give you a medal,' I said excitedly. But I could tell he was unimpressed.

'Tsars—revolutionaries: nothing they do matters to me. First and foremost I am a scientist, concerned with finding the truth.'

Realizing that this might have sounded a little pompous, he playfully tugged my cap to the side and said, 'Well, young man, any questions?'

'I have one, sir. Why wait till now to tell me all this when, begging your pardon, sir, you would hardly breathe a word of it before?'

'I wanted to make sure we were safely aboard the *Ursus* first.'

'Did you think I might run off when I found out?'

'I'm not sure. Probably. You see, Yanis, I haven't quite given you the complete picture yet.' He watched my face closely. 'When we get to Osva—to the prison—one of the prisoners being held there, and one we shall certainly meet is—' His eyes flickered to mine, '—Nikolay Kolchak. He was captured a couple of weeks after that old newspaper headline and condemned to death for treason. The same Nikolay Kolchak who Mrs Pafnutkin stuffed your head with so much nonsense about when you were at the orphanage . . . Now do you understand?'

Saying nothing, I chewed my lip.

'I'm sorry, Yanis, it's not in my nature to be so deceitful, but I'd already lost one assistant, I could not run the risk of losing another. Are you angry with me? In the end I cannot force you to come with me, we stop at many ports along the way.'

I met his gaze directly.

'Does it bother you, sir, that we shall see the Tsar's great enemy locked up in his cell?'

He looked surprised.

'No . . . Why on earth should it?'

'Then, sir, it doesn't bother me either. And I

would never have run away and missed the chance of sailing with you on the *Ursus*, no matter where we went or who we saw.'

I wanted to find out more about the doctor's various instruments and how they worked, and he was pleased to show me. He started with the drawers of callipers, used, I was told, for measuring thickness and distances across the head. The smallest was the size of my little finger, while the largest was spring-loaded and multi-armed and might easily have been mistaken for an instrument of torture.

'For measuring circumferences of skulls,' he explained, ghoulishly snapping it at me.

Then he showed me an ophthalmoscope, for inspecting the eye, and a magic lantern packed up with boxes of slides all carefully marked and dated. When I enquired as to what the labels said, he pointed to a few, reading out such things as *The North-Eastern Pomeranian nose: a general overview . . . The under-developed fluted nostril—case studies . . . The right inverse snout—the Ginsburg family, Danzig.*

'What?' I laughed. 'You have pictures of people's noses?'

'The collection, I believe, is unrivalled.'

However, Dr Gomarus's main joy was reserved for his camera (the disassembled machine I had seen earlier). When put together on a tripod, it resembled a miniature brass cannon, but the doctor assured me he had no interest in blowing heads off bodies. Where was the science in that? No, he wanted to photograph them. At Osva, he told me, it was his intention to photograph each prisoner twice—once from the front, once from the side.

'This is where you come in, Yanis. Your chief duty will be to develop these photographs after I have taken them.'

My eyes widened.

'Me, sir? But how?'

Dr Gomarus nodded in the direction of the cabinet of crystals and liquids.

'Everything you need is in that one box. It isn't magic. If you correctly follow each stage and measure out the right quantities, and if you are careful and patient and mindful of the occasional danger, then I see no reason why you can't rise to the job as well as my last assistant.'

I wasn't so sure.

'But, *sir*, it'll be too difficult. I don't think I can!'

'Nonsense. You have an intelligent head on your shoulders, boy, it's the truth—it's why I chose you and not that big, dull, blond lad . . . Ah, but I can tell you are going to take some convincing in this matter. Very well, let me convince you, we have plenty of time, so why wait till we reach Osva? Boy, put on an apron, I am going to start your training straight away.'

My complete ignorance of photography meant that my training had to begin at the very beginning . . .

Lesson one: taking the photograph.

Dressed in his over-large coat and hat and fur mittens, Dr Gomarus set up his camera out on deck. He hoped our fellow passengers could be lured out to pose for him; he hoped they would brave the cold—at least for as long as it took to sit on the hard, wooden stool he had placed at exactly the right angle in front of the rail and smile. However, no sooner was the camera on its tripod than two grim-faced men in black coats marched up, a worried-looking steward in tow a few paces behind.

'You there—why is this stretch of river of so much interest to you?'

The question genuinely took Dr Gomarus by surprise. He peered over his shoulder at the frozen river as if noticing it for the first time.

'River? No . . . you have it all wrong. It's people I want to photograph.'

'But with the river in the background?'

'Why . . . yes . . . I suppose.'

'It is simply not permitted.'

'You will give us your name.' The second man sounded no friendlier than the first.

Unprotesting, Dr Gomarus gave his name, then gave mine (well, the name of his old assistant). Both were written down in a note-book, along with an address Dr Gomarus was obliged to give.

'You will put away that camera immediately and move along.'

'I see . . . well, if I must.'

The two black-coated men turned and marched off. The steward dashed after them and managed to reach the door in time to open it. The men swept through. On the deck above, I noticed Miss Mirsky hovering at a half-opened door on First. She must have witnessed everything, and I saw how her mouth was pressed into a thin-lipped smile.

The steward made his way back to us, sheep-ishly hanging his head, his hands raised to show the spotless white palms of his gloves.

'What can I say, gentlemen? It appears some-body has made a complaint.'

Guessing who it was, I jerked my head up, a ready-made scowl on my face, but Miss Mirsky had conveniently slipped away inside.

'Complaint indeed,' said Dr Gomarus. 'What is there to complain about in something so innocent as taking photographs?'

'I'm sorry, sir, rules aboard the *Ursus* are pretty strict, even those rules you never hear about unless you happen to break them.'

'Hmm.'

Dr Gomarus carefully unscrewed the lens of his camera and polished it with a cloth. The steward lingered, keen to make amends. He looked about him like a third-rate spy.

'But there are ways and means, sir, even aboard the *Ursus* . . . If you're still keen on taking your photographs and don't mind the sort it is, sir, might I suggest you try your luck in steerage. Nobody bothers much with what goes on down there. And a lot of folk set up stalls and businesses. You know the type—toothpullers, pie sellers, hair trimmers. You wouldn't appear out of place. I have a pass key—if you like, I could let you down there.'

Dr Gomarus caught my eye.

'What do you say, Yanis, you up to a visit below stairs?'

Keen to see another part of the ship, I nodded eagerly.

The steward smiled and seemed almost relieved.

'Then if you gentlemen would kindly follow me . . .'

Dr Gomarus carried his camera, the tripod angled carefully over his shoulder; the steward was entrusted with the empty box, and I carried the stool.

The steward led us to the nearest service stairs and we went down them until, at the bottom, a metal door blocked our way.

'There is a bell on the other side, sir,' explained the steward taking out his keys. 'Ring for me when you are done and I will let you back up.'

Then he pushed open the door and we were into steerage.

At first my eyes couldn't adapt to the smoky darkness, and the noise was as if from a busy street market. And as the three of us stood there, unsure, on the edge of this strange teeming underworld, a harsh voice called out to us.

'Close that door, damn you, or I'll come over there and knock off your hats. You're letting out all the heat!'

The threat of violence was enough to scare off our helpful steward friend.

'Remember the bell, sir, when you wish to

return.' And with that he was gone, slamming the door behind him.

Dr Gomarus pushed up his hat from his brow. 'Now what?' I asked.

'Come on, we'll find ourselves a quiet little corner somewhere.'

Doubting whether such a thing existed, I sighed, picked up the abandoned box, and followed him.

The noise immediately closed around us. It came not only from the hundreds of people, but also their livestock, which moved freely wherever it wished. This being the lower part of the ship, the rumble and vibration from the ice-runners was also much greater; it was there behind all the other sounds, so that the fetid air palpably throbbed.

By now my eyes were grown used to the smoke and lack of light. I saw that, unlike the decks above, the ship's construction—the rivets and girders—hadn't been hidden away behind decorative panelling. And there were no electric lights or radiators. The smoke that caught the back of my throat came mostly from communal brick ovens, which were the main source of heat. Passengers in steerage did not have meals supplied by smart waiters in restaurants, they had to bring their own food and cook it themselves—that was the way of things when travelling on a cheap ticket.

Yet these ovens were simply the biggest I had ever seen, the size of furnaces, with many people crowded on top like nesting seagulls, taking advantage of the rising heat. Elsewhere, instead of cabins, I noticed tiny stalls occupied by many members of the same family, their only means of privacy a ragged curtain pulled across the front; and they peered out through the holes, like territorial creatures guarding their burrows.

Apart from the ovens, smoke also came from clay pipes smoked by an astonishing number of those in steerage—men, women, and even older children; though the lower rank soldiers returning from leave preferred to roll spindly cigarettes, each squaddie puffing his down to his bright orange knuckles. They (the soldiers) squatted down on their haunches to play cards on upturned buckets, their blasphemies quite shocking, and I wondered, did no one dare object and ask them to stop? The women in headscarves pretended not to hear them as they knelt on the floor kneading dough, pausing to rub flour off their noses with the backs of their hands, or to glance sideways at their toddling babies, comical in baggy nappies. And if it happened that one of the babies took a tumble and fell, he knew better than to howl for his busy mama, but managed to find his own feet again by hauling himself up the side of an animal, coarse, grey, goat hair clenched in fat determined baby fists.

In all this, Dr Gomarus at last managed to find us a corner that, if not completely quiet, was at least unoccupied, our arrival hardly raising a glimmer of interest from those around.

'If I just put my camera down here a moment. Well . . . yes. Good-day to everyone. Madam—excuse me—if I may be so bold as to ask you to move that crate. That's the one . . . many thanks, dear lady.'

He set up his camera and stool, pacing out the distance between them; and once satisfied with this, he turned bravely to the crowd—which by now had lost what little interest it had in us and what we were doing—and called, 'Might I crave your indulgence, good people. My name is Gomarus and I humbly ask that one of you would step forward and be my volunteer.'

'*Volunteer*,' said a passing soldier sourly. 'In the army the first thing you learn is not to volunteer for anything.'

'Quite so. But as I'm not a military man there is absolutely no danger of anyone getting shot. I need a volunteer who will sit for me and at no expense have his or her photographic portrait taken. You have all seen a camera before?'

They hadn't. They were ordinary folk. Why should anyone want to take a photograph of them? But word spread quickly and we drew a size-able crowd and from it stepped—or was pushed— a thin, awkward-looking fellow, slipping off his cap in frightened respect.

'If you promise it won't hurt, master . . .'

'*Hurt*. Why on earth should it hurt?' laughed Dr Gomarus. 'No, please, take yourself forward and sit on the stool, and whatever you do, don't move until I say so.'

The man obeyed him as slavishly as he obeyed anyone with an air of authority. I watched him stretch open his eyes in an effort not to blink. The effect was so comic I wanted to laugh. Dr Gomarus meanwhile had gone behind the camera and thrust his head beneath a black cloth.

'Perfectly still, remember.'

The doctor's hand came snaking out to remove the lens cap. Then I heard him slowly begin to count what he called his exposure time.

'One . . . two . . . three . . .'

As he came up to forty, the man's nerve finally broke and he leapt to his feet, panic-stricken.

'Sorry, master. Sorry. I can't do it. It just don't seem natural somehow.'

Dr Gomarus's head re-emerged from under the black cloth, staring at him uncomprehendingly.

'What are you doing? Sit down, man. You have just ruined a perfectly good plate.'

But words alone were not enough to persuade the fellow to do anything other than stand moon-eyed and rigid, gripping his cap tightly in his hands. The crowd gave a murmur of sympathy, and Dr Gomarus was forced to desert his camera and ease him back into place, gently but firmly pushing him down by his shoulders. However, from sheer force of habit, he couldn't resist running his fingers over his sitter's head, moving them in a circular motion upon his temples.

'That's interesting.'

'What is, master?'

'In later life you will be prone to bouts of rheumatic fever.'

'That sounds awful bad, master.'

'Not really.' Dr Gomarus traced an invisible line across the top of his skull. 'You have an over-sized heart and will be lucky to live much past fifty.'

'*Fifty, master!* But I turned forty-eight last June.'

Depressed, the man slumped down upon the stool.

'Perfect,' declared Dr Gomarus hurrying back and loading a new plate.

Around me I felt the crowd surge as if changing feet and a whisper passed amongst it.

'That educated fellow—he's a bit of a fortune-teller. Why didn't he say so to begin with?'

At last they thought they understood the true nature of Dr Gomarus's work, and when his first volunteer staggered off, ashen faced, pushing blindly through the crowd, the doctor had no shortage of others willing to take his place. He took six more photographs after that—three of labourers, one of a tipsy soldier, one of a mother and her child, and lastly a small girl with a turn in her eye.

'That's all I have time for today,' he said taking the small girl by the hand and leading her back to her mother; and to me he said, 'There, Yanis, my part is all done. Now it is your turn.'

I surprised myself.

Under the doctor's supervision I rose to his challenge.

By the end of the afternoon I had hung seven new black and white photographic prints on the cabin wall.

Unsmiling, like the saints in church, warning me not to be too proud.

But I *was* proud, and when Dr Gomarus jokingly referred to the photographs as a rogues' gallery, I laughed with self-satisfied pleasure.

That night, as usual, I knelt to say my prayers.

'God bless the Tsar,
Keep him strong and in health,
and thoroughly scoured until spotless
God bless the Tsarina,
May she . . .
be held by the bottom to prevent unwanted fingerprints
God bless the little Tsarevich,
And his sisters the imperial princesses,
kept in darkness to avoid over-exposure
God watch over our government,
otherwise known as the fixing agent
And keep us safe . . .
and stored away in cotton-wool
. . . from our enemies.
God bless me,
making sure no noxious fumes leak out
And help me serve Dr Gomarus and be the best photographer's assistant there has ever been.

Amen.'

We were now four days away from the orphanage
(although it seemed more like four years) and my
time aboard the *Ursus* had already settled into a
routine of serving Dr Gomarus and perfecting
my skills as his assistant. In the mornings we went
down together into steerage, the doctor having
become a familiar figure there with his tripod and
camera slung over his shoulder, and from each
photographic plate he took, I—returning alone to
our cabin—developed a photograph, which was
duly presented to the sitter the following day. For
this, Dr Gomarus did not ask so much as a thank-
you, so our appearance on the lower deck always
caused something of a stir. In fact we became so
badly mobbed that in the end Dr Gomarus had
no other choice than to charge half a dracul a
sitting. Even so we remained wildly popular.

As for my own progress, Dr Gomarus pronounced himself most pleased with it. He said I
had a good brain and that I learned quickly. And
he grew more eager than ever that I should be
able to read and write. Somehow it offended him
that I could not understand names on labels, but
was forced to recognize various chemicals by the

shapes of their bottles or the colour of the mixture within. His lessons began soon after, in the afternoons when we had more free time. But the doctor was an impatient teacher. For him, being able to read and write was something he took for granted—like breathing.

How he sighed and drummed his fingers at my slowness.

Sometimes he got up to pace the floor.

This made me more nervous and clumsy than ever, and I wished we could be at Osmabinsk, the last of the upriver cities. At Osmabinsk the doctor had promised to go ashore and buy me some practice books so I could work alone at my own pace. After Osmabinsk, he said, there was hardly anything but snow, forest, and wild animals. This set me wondering about the Countess. What did she dread most, the packs of wolves or the long winter days in the company of Miss Mirsky?

If it were me, I knew how I would answer.

Osmabinsk was spotted just after noon, its place in the distance marked by eight industrial chimneys leaking dirty yellow smoke into an otherwise clear sky. However, we had to wait several more hours before the rest of the city was sighted. When it was, it came into view all at once.

Meantime it hinted at its presence: telegraph poles, leaning drunkenly in different directions, appeared over the brow of a hill and commenced to follow the course of the river; then came a municipal rubbish dump, the sky above it patrolled by screeching seagulls. Several snowy villages came and went, with scattered villas in between. And the forest all but disappeared, either cut down or neatened into gardens. Ahead a sharp bend in the river.

As soon as it was sighted, a bell rang summoning teams of crew on deck, and the teams, keeping to their tight formations, went scrambling up the rigging to lower all but the topmost sails, slowing the progress of the ski-ship markedly. Fishermen, alerted to us by vibrations, looked up from their holes in the ice and waved. Then the banks of snow seemed to drift apart like frozen billows, and there was Osmabinsk, a sprawling dreary city of old wooden warehouses and ugly new tenement blocks, little hemmed-in churches, and government buildings pretending to be shrunken palaces. The tenements were already slums, every balcony hung with washing or piled up with junk or firewood. Some balconies were converted into pigeon lofts, others given over to the family dog, the dogs standing fearlessly on their parapets, barking at each other or at the sky.

As the ship sailed closer, I started to make out the waterfront; horse-drawn trams moving with dream-like speed along a wide riverside boulevard. Closer still and I could watch ski-barges being unloaded of grain; the great grabbing cranes, that rose and descended like monsters feeding on the innards of their prey. The city snow was grey and the river ice yellow. Youths sailed ski-kayaks. And the smell off the city was like a dog's damp coat.

Standing out on deck, I took immense pleasure in all these things. The weather was mild enough to induce a thaw—that is, if the irregular drip of melt water counted as a proper thaw, for all it did was pit the lying snow. Still, I hadn't bothered with my cap and the breeze struck my skin more wet than cold.

Turning again in the direction of the city, I noticed teams of haulers making their way out onto the ice—not convicts this time but the lowliest of dock workers. With their hunched shoulders and pinched raw faces, their sack-padded jackets and spiked iron boots, they looked no different.

The command to lower all sails was given. The *Ursus* slithered to a halt. Taking up their ropes, the haulers dragged the ship to an empty pier and, as they did so, the decks began filling with those about to disembark.

Ten minutes later we docked next to the port-master's little brick office. He—the port-master—could be seen through a window, surrounded by cabinets and tottering piles of ledgers, which created the impression he had much to do. But there he sat quite at ease by his fire, smoking a pipe and reading a newspaper; he did not even turn his head to see the *Ursus* come in and be secured.

Leaving him to enjoy his peace, I studied the outside wall of his office where the same patriotic poster had been pasted up many times. It was a picture of the Tsar towering over a slogan in thick black ink. The fact I could recognize some of the letters excited me, and turning to the woman by my side I asked her what the slogan said. She looked quite startled by my ignorance.

' "One God, one Tsar, one people", of course.'

She answered me so shortly that I could not be bothered to thank her. Instead, I wondered who had made the Tsar cross-eyed, and given him extra large ears and vampire fangs dripping with blood.

Disembarkation was a very noisy bad-tempered business. It seemed the whole ship wanted to get off at Osmabinsk, but it was not proving easy. The gangways were too narrow, and porters who pushed up them went against the flow, and smiling stewards, who lingered after tips, clogged them at the top. Luggage was held head high, and hats knocked askew, and toes trampled, and furious words exchanged.

The crush might have been worse in steerage, but it was impossible to say, as its passengers got off at a much lower level, *underneath* the pier. And although out of sight, I could hear the bleats of their frightened animals, and through gaps in the pier's planking I was able to make out a general shuffling movement away from the ship; at the same time, a powerful farmyard smell rose from the opened doors.

And all the while, with so much going on, I kept a steady watch on the upper deck. Still the Countess hadn't appeared. She said she was going all the way to Osva so there was no reason why she should, but what if something had happened? What if Miss Mirsky had drugged her or locked her in a cupboard? What if—

'Yanis! Yanis!'

I heard Dr Gomarus calling me.

'Yes, doctor?'

Dr Gomarus was oddly agitated.

'Come here, I wish to speak to you. The secret police will be coming aboard soon to check everyone's papers.'

'But the soldiers have done ours already.'

'It makes no difference, it's their job to do it again. And with Osva our next port of call, security's tight. Now, do you remember the name of my old assistant?'

I shrugged. 'Goshka something.'

'*Goshka something simply will not do*—do you want to land us both in prison? His name was Goshka *Kulich*. Say it—'

'Goshka Kulich.'

'Don't forget.'

I wouldn't—not like he had forgotten his promise to go into Osmabinsk to buy me some practice books. Frowning with displeasure, he turned and went back inside while I remained a little longer on deck. With the last few passengers drifting away, I saw a small group of men in long leather coats and carrying attaché cases march purposefully towards the ship.

I was not the only one to notice.

Inside his office, the port-master was frantically signing forms, his newspaper and pipe nowhere in sight.

Outside, new posters covered the defaced ones.

At six-thirty we were summoned to the third class smoking-room after waiting in our cabin for the call. It had been an uncomfortable wait, Dr Gomarus growing more and more edgy and making me so; and then, when we finally reached the portside room, he nearly tripped over me in the doorway. We entered. Inside, the air was disagreeably fuggy with old tobacco smoke. Immediately I spotted two men at the room's furthest end, lounging easily on one of the sofas. Both still wore their long black coats, tightly done up; the first, hearing us come in, briefly glanced down at a sheaf of papers scattered between him and his colleague.

'That's right—come right in, *Dr Gomarus. Ha-ha-ha*. We don't want you catching your deaths out there.'

He motioned to two chairs in front of the sofa and we sat down. Dr Gomarus crossed his legs, uncrossed them, then clasped his hands in his lap, twiddling his thumbs.

The second secret policeman leaned across and whispered something into the first one's ear.

'So, interesting—interesting. You are a scientist, Dr Gomarus? Going to Osva?'

'That is correct.'

'*Ha-ha-ha*. Relax, doctor, we shan't eat you, you have nothing to fear . . . Now, may we see your papers, please?' He rolled his eyes as if sharing a joke. 'I tell you there is so much paperwork in this job.'

Dr Gomarus took out his papers and offered them to him, but it was the other secret policeman who took them. He quickly scanned them, then whispered a second time into his colleague's ear.

'Ah, I think you own a camera, doctor.'

'Yes.'

'You like taking pictures?'

'*Photographs*. Yes. It is part of my work.'

'You work on the *Ursus*?'

'No.'

'*Ha-ha-ha*. So you take pictures for pleasure too. Little souvenirs of your journey perhaps?'

Dr Gomarus shifted uncomfortably.

'That was a misunderstanding. I explained to the—'

'*Ha-ha-ha*. A little thing. No matter—no matter.'

I noticed that whenever he laughed, the eyes of the secret policeman remained watchful and utterly cold.

His colleague whispered again and the police-man turned his measured smile on me.

95

'Ah. *Ha-ha-ha.* You are Master Goshka Kulich, I believe?'

I nodded.

'You work for the doctor?'

Nod.

'And you are also travelling to Osva?'

Nod.

'Tell me, Goshka Kulich, are you a good boy?'

Unsure what to say I turned to the doctor.

'He's a very g—'

'*Let him speak, doctor . . . Ha-ha-ha.* Let young Master Kulich answer for himself—*please.*'

My voice seemed to stick in my dried-up throat.

'I . . . I hope so, sir.'

'Good—good.'

He leant forward studying my face.

'And do you love the Tsar?'

'Yes, sir.'

'Do you love him with all your heart?'

'Yes, sir.'

'*Ha-ha-ha.* Good—good. And tell me, Goshka Kulich, do you know all the words to "Our beloved country—our beloved Tsar"?'

I felt Dr Gomarus staring at me, almost willing me to give the right answer.

'Yes, sir, I do, sir.'

'*Ha-ha-ha,* you hear that?' said the man to his whispering companion. 'The patriotic boy knows

96

all the words. Excellent—excellent. Perhaps we should put him to the test.'

And with that he got up, crossed to the next table and, with one sweep of his arm, cleared it of newspapers and ashtrays; the ashtrays rattling across the wooden floor. This unexpected burst of violence startled and confused me, especially when he turned to me with a friendly smile upon his face.

'Come—come.'

He beckoned me forwards with his fingers.

I didn't want to go, but felt Dr Gomarus's hand in the small of my back, propelling me, and knew there was no escape. I approached the man slowly. 'A big clear voice,' he said helping me up onto the table.

So there I stood, exposed to three sets of eyes, feeling foolish and frightened and awkward.

'Well, Master Kulich? *Ha-ha-ha.* Your audience is growing impatient.'

In a voice hardly more than a whisper I began. 'O'er the proud eagle—'

'Louder . . . ! Much louder.'

'O'er the proud eagle
The angels watch over
A corner of Heaven
Men claim for their own.
The snows on the mountains
Slow waters through meadows:

We the glad children
The Tsar calls his own.'

By the end of the verse, I was singing more confidently, my voice, if I say so myself, not such a bad one.

I started the second verse, the policeman joining in and nearly drowning me out with his booming bass. Then the whispering policeman rocketed to his feet and added *his* voice, his hand on his chest against his heart. This left only Dr Gomarus seated. He blinked in bewilderment. Then he too stood up, his voice thin and tuneless and tinged with embarrassment.

'And should storm clouds gather,
With our blood we promise
To stand firm together
And protect the throne.
His foe is our foe,
His breath is our breath:
One people, one Tsar,
One God, and one home.'

There were no more questions. The quiet one stamped our papers (and I swear on the head of my mother—whoever she is—there were tears in his eyes), then we were casually dismissed—me with a pinch on the cheek and a two dracul piece pressed into my hand.

Outside on deck, the sharp clear air gave me a sudden headache; Dr Gomarus slumped against the ship's rail.

'Oh, Yanis . . .' He took off his pink spectacles and rubbed his eyes. 'I suppose we have Mrs Pafnutkin to thank for your word-perfect rendering of the Tsar's song?'

'Yes, sir, at the orphanage we sang it on important saints' days, as well as on the Tsar's birthday and naming day. She was afraid that—'

'An official would come from the Town Hall and accuse her of being unpatriotic.'

'Yes, sir. But how did you know that?'

He managed a smile.

'An intelligent guess—still, hurrah, I say, for Madam Pafnutkin. And at least the ordeal's behind us. Come on, Yanis, I'm suddenly in need of a drink, and you must be famished.'

The cheaper restaurant on third class was empty, the waiters slouched over the counter near the samovar, whispering and giggling together, one curling the hair in front of his ear into a kiss-curl. No one came over to show us to a table, it didn't seem worth their effort: we could see for ourselves that every place was available.

'Here will do us just fine,' decided Dr Gomarus unbuttoning his coat.

We sat down, Dr Gomarus straight away tucking a napkin into his collar in readiness.

I gazed around with cowed head. Although less formal than the one on Second, I found the restaurant a curiously joyless place, its mirrored walls painted over with scenes of a sunny seaside village, its paper lanterns shabby and unlit.

Usually we did not come to places like this, usually we ate alone in our cabin, an arrangement that suited us both well. Dr Gomarus didn't like crowds (not a problem tonight); and I fretted in situations like this for not knowing how things were. Back at the orphanage, mealtimes had been simple affairs. We each had a wooden bowl, and spoon, and the fingers God gave us. But here I was presented with a whole burglar's hoard of knives and forks, and expected to know which to choose. And it was not just the cutlery! There was one type of cup for coffee, another for tea; one type of glass for water, another for wine; one type of container for salt, another for sugar . . . And what on earth were you supposed to say when asked the impossible question—what would you like to eat?

The first time we had dined at an on-board restaurant, Dr Gomarus had had to stop me from licking my plate. He reached out and touched my wrist, saying gently, 'While it is logical to lick one's plate clean, it isn't a done thing in public.' And I was aware that around us people were staring, some laughing behind menus and hands, and I burned with shame.

I blushed at the memory of it even now.

Eventually a waiter bothered to tear himself away from his friends and came slouching over. He handed Dr Gomarus a menu and stood impatiently tapping his pad with his pencil.

'The eel for me . . . and, Yanis, how about the soup?' He knew I could just about cope with that, and he ordered extra bread. 'And bring me an apricot brandy—a *large* one.'

I followed the waiter with my eyes as he walked away. He said something to his friends (perhaps about the doctor's odd spectacles) that made them glance our way and laugh; and I found myself admiring his crisp white jacket, seeing it had been so perfectly starched.

The waiter returned carrying the brandy on a tray, his free hand behind his back like a dancer, and not many minutes later the food followed. The soup was celery—lukewarm and growing a skin on top.

We began to eat.

'How is your soup?' enquired Dr Gomarus.

'Good . . . And your eel?'

'Boney.'

The outside door opened and, glad for a moment's diversion, we both looked round. The figure who entered wore the trademark long black coat of a secret policeman, but was obviously a cadet, hardly older than the waiters who called out to him and laughingly beckoned him over.

He undid his coat and casually slipped his hands into his trouser pockets. He grinned, his teeth uneven. 'How's life going for you boys in the exciting world of table-waiting?' he asked with good-natured sarcasm.

His appearance enlivened the waiters' conversation, making it louder and more boisterous. They boasted about girls they said they knew. Then one plucked at the police-cadet's coat and asked whether he was carrying a firearm tonight.

He shrugged coyly.

'Maybe.'

He glanced round, decided we were of no importance, and pulled out a long-barrelled revolver.

Thoroughly impressed, the waiters took turns holding it. '*Ke-pow—Ke-pow*.' They fired pretend bullets at their reflections in the mirrored walls, trying to beat them on the draw.

'You ever shot anyone with this?'

The cadet took up a swaggering stance against the counter. 'One . . . maybe two, you know . . .'

'*Two people*. You shot two people?'

'Hey, keep your voice down, idiot. Now give the gun to me before the chief comes sniffing round. It's not standard issue, he'll have a fit if he knows I've got it.'

He took the gun, slipped it back inside his coat and they returned to the safe topic of girls. Dr Gomarus and I continued to eat. We had gone too long without speaking, and now the restaurant seemed to grow uncomfortably large around us, like a mirrored cavern, and I winced at the dull scrape my spoon made on the bottom of my dish. I wished we could just leave. Then, from outside, came a sound that made us all lift our heads and listen more closely.

'Someone's letting off fireworks,' said our waiter sauntering across to our table. He wasn't speaking to us, though, and collected up our dishes in silence. Outside, the distant crackling was heard again.

The cadet stiffened like a pointer.

'That isn't fireworks. It's gunfire!'

'It can't be.'

'I tell you, that's gunfire!'

The cadet led the dash to the nearest landside window; our waiter, abandoning his pile of dirty dishes and his dignity, flew across and joined them.

The crackling sound, although distant, had become continuous.

'*There—there*. I think I saw something—like sparks over the rooftops. Let's go outside and see.'

The little group, thinking and moving as one, rushed to the door, leaving it wide open; and it was the cold draught more than anything which finally persuaded Dr Gomarus it was time for us to go. He threw down his napkin and some coins and pulled on his coat.

'Come on, Yanis, let's find out if this song and dance is warranted.'

'Do you think it really is gunfire, doctor?'

He shrugged and pushed his chair under the table.

Outside, there was considerable excitement. A large building was ablaze on the edge of the city, the flames curling up in long elegant fronds, lighting other buildings around it with a muted orange glow. The waiters jabbered and whooped as if spectators at some sort of entertainment. We stood apart from them, and instinctively and protectively I glanced up at the deck above. As I did, a jolt went through me. I saw a figure glide out of the shadows and knew at once it was the Countess.

I thought how fearless and brave she was, for far from shrinking back, she moved forward to the ship's rail, her face all the while turned towards the fire. I studied her. She wore a dark hood and cloak; and although her features were half in shadow, a drop diamond hanging from each ear caught the ship's lights and sparkled as brilliantly as melt water. She held her hands before her, buried deep in the warmth of a fur muff, and, as I continued to watch, I saw her take out a strange pair of glasses (opera glasses as I now know them to be) and calmly hold them up to her eyes.

Nobody else noticed her there all alone on First, and I was overcome by an urge to call to her, to tell her not to worry, when I heard a shrill whistling sound—then silence—and out on the river came a startling red flash. Dr Gomarus winced and covered his eyes. A second later we heard the ice groan and felt a shudder rising up through the decks.

We rushed to the opposite rail.

Out on the ice a black mark had appeared as if a sack of soot had been dropped from a great height, at its centre a half-filled crater of water.

'Hell,' said the waiter next to me, 'they're attacking us. Those bloodthirsty pigs are actually firing on the *Ursus*.'

Hearing this, I began to tremble. The danger was real and undeniable, we might be blown to pieces at any moment . . . But instead of feverishly saying my prayers, I wanted to laugh out loud. I wanted to run up and down the length of the ship, shouting at the top of my voice. The cold night air on my face, the hot smoky breath around me . . . really, I wanted to laugh, I'd never felt so alive; and if I trembled it was only out of a wild kind of excitement.

Then the restaurant doors burst open and there was a babble of new voices as our little group was swollen by cooks and kitchen hands who, alarmed at the violent rattling of pots and plates, had come to find out what was going on, some still clutching ladles and cleavers.

'Do you think they're trying to sink us?' asked one when the shell-hole was pointed out to him.

'They don't have to,' said Dr Gomarus with quiet authority. 'If they manage to break the ice, that is enough. By morning the *Ursus* will be frozen into the river and quite unable to move until the spring-time thaw.'

The cadet blazed with fury.

'See how dirty they fight us—this is not a civilized war.'

As he finished speaking, we heard the shrill whistling sound again, and recognizing it for what it was, instinctively ducked. Another blood-red flash tore through the darkness, the force of the explosion knocking me back a step.

One of the waiters swore. Another wiped the sweat off his brow with his sleeve.

'Mother of God, that was close.'

'They're trying to kill us!'

'They're determined . . .'

'Well, the captain can go down with his ship if he likes—but not me. Not on my wages! Anyone with me?'

Four or five of the restaurant staff turned to make a dash for the nearest gangway.

'Hold fast, you men!'

A harsh female voice halted them in their tracks. Everyone looked up to see who had made such a bellow. It was Miss Mirsky. She had pushed in front of the Countess, and was pointing down with a small silver pistol.

'Now listen to me. You will all remain at your posts. You will show yourselves loyal to his majesty. Desertion will not be tolerated. Anyone who tries will be dealt a coward's death with a bullet in his back. And don't think being a woman I won't do it, because I promise you I shall.'

And to prove she really meant what she said, she fired her gun into the air. I jumped in surprise and felt my neck click.

A third shell whistled over our heads and exploded on the ice, the nearest one yet. Everyone stood still, not knowing what to do; but it hardly seemed to matter what we decided now, for we found ourselves overtaken by events on the pier. There, like worker insects serving a great queen, swarms of police ran everywhere, pulling away gangways, untying ropes; and out on the river others were marshalling themselves into teams. Aboard ship, sailors scrambled up the rigging, not in teams in their usual showmanlike way, but at the double, and as soon as they burst up on deck, some without hats or coats.

'We're setting sail,' gasped one of the waiters hearing the flap of sailcloth.

Out on the river, I watched the police teams take up ropes and begin to pull. Without benefit of spiked boots, there was always one or other of their number slipping over, which made them appear both clownish and desperate. Wind filled the sails and the *Ursus* inched forward, scraping its side along the pier, gathering speed. Voices shouted out in the dark. Then a fourth shell lit up the scene like a bolt of lightning.

But we were moving fast now—out into the open river and safety.

The priggish young cadet, bursting with patriotism, turned and saluted the efforts of those back at port.

'That shows God is on our side,' he growled. 'He wouldn't let those filthy traitors humiliate our Tsar. He wouldn't let them harm our great Tsar's ship.'

'Long live the Tsar!' cheered the cooks and waiters, as if they had had a hand in winning the moment and conveniently forgetting how close some had been to jumping ship.

I glanced up at the higher deck. Miss Mirsky was ushering the Countess away. This time, when I saw something reflecting the ship's lights, it wasn't the Countess's diamonds, but the small 'lady's' pistol tightly gripped in Miss Mirsky's capable hand.

We eventually stopped some five or six miles upriver, less because it was an ideal distance away from the city and the revolutionaries' guns, and more because it might prove perilous pressing ahead without so much as a star to guide us. With the order given, sails were struck for a second time that day, and the great white and gold mailship slid to an eerie halt between banks of impenetrable snowy forest. As an extra precaution, the passengers (those few of us who remained) were ordered to return to our cabins and lock ourselves in. Half an hour later the generators were switched off and the ship was plunged into darkness, without light or heat. We stumbled around blindly trying to find our nightshirts, Dr Gomarus deciding that an early night might be the very thing after so much excitement.

However, even if I had wanted to, I could not sleep. The soldiers in steerage had been allowed out to patrol the decks, which they did without guns or discipline, managing to break into one of the stores and get themselves staggeringly drunk. All night long they kept up their noise, kicking doors, cursing, arguing with the secret policemen, and fighting the sailors.

We lay in our bunks listening to them.

'Sometimes, what idiotic creatures we humans are,' I heard Dr Gomarus mutter under his breath.

Surprisingly, by next morning, the *Ursus* was able to continue its journey as if nothing had happened: the broken glass must have been cleared up at first light and the decks put back in order— the only reminder of the previous day being a length of twisted rail from the ship's collision with the pier at Osmabinsk.

Dr Gomarus and I did not venture down into steerage that morning as was our custom, the doctor judging it unwise. 'Too many sore heads and short tempers and unsettled scores for my liking.' So he stayed in bed, wearing his coat and scarf, a book propped up upon his chest, leaving me to amuse myself however I wished. A little later he peered over his pink spectacles and asked what I was doing.

'Practising my handwriting, sir. Is the sound of the nib disturbing you?'

'Oh, no—no. Not at all. You go ahead.'

Now he had broken the silence, I said, 'Do you think the revolutionaries might attack us again?'

'Who can say? It's like knowing the mind of a fox. Perhaps.' He read on a few more lines. 'Are you worried in case they do?'

'No.'

'You didn't seem frightened last night.'

'I wasn't.'

I put down my pen and got up; I stretched and slipped on my coat.

'Where are you going?'

'Outside . . . for some fresh air, sir.'

He didn't look up from his book.

'You spend a lot of time out on deck, don't you, Yanis?'

His words seemed to me to be heavy with other meaning. I quickly mumbled something and dashed for the door.

We sailed north-east, the river growing narrower, the hours of daylight shorter; and the Northern Lights coolly ablaze in the midnight sky. Distant mountains became our travelling companions, and it snowed hard every day so that almost the first chore on board was to clear it away, even from the spars and masts before the crew could hoist the sails. The temperature dropped still further as we crossed into the Aznoya region, and the cold was a dry cold that gnawed at your bones. I was warned not to spend more than an hour out on deck or risk frostbite. But the cold didn't bother me. Passing a mirror, I saw how it had cracked and scabbed my lips. They bled whenever I spoke.

And yet there was so much I wanted to see and to see it all demanded patience. It was only by spending time out on deck that I noticed how the snow kept changing; seeing too that it was not always white—as at sunset when the whole vast landscape glowed the warmest shade of pink. And once, standing alone, I saw a bear—a white bear—thin and miserable and scavenging along the shore. I shouted to it and waved my cap, and it raised its greasy muzzle in salute.

It was only when I went inside I thought of other things.

That night in my bunk I wondered about the Countess. I wondered if it was only the cold that prevented her from stepping out in public. I wondered if Miss Mirsky paced angrily about their cabin on First, her pistol at her side . . . And I wondered if I would catch sight of either woman tomorrow when we reached Osva, our last port of call.

We finally arrived just after the noon bell, the day being cold but brilliantly sunny; and I have to say now, Osva was nothing like I was expecting.

In my mind I had often imagined it as something rather special, after all it was the last stop at the end of a thousand mile journey which few were allowed to complete. So I was expecting domes and silver towers. I was expecting a city mysteriously looming out of the mist. I was expecting flags and trumpets and ringing bells . . . Not so.

My voice rose shrilly in the thin icy air.

'But there's nothing here!'

In my disappointment I sounded angry—as though I'd been cheated. I stood with the doctor out on deck, surrounded by polished mahogany boxes—above us the *Ursus*'s sails all struck, its masts as bare as winter trees. Ten minutes ago the ship had ground to a halt at some vague point slightly closer to the left bank—this, I was told, was Osva; although there was not a single rooftop or chimney to be seen.

'Nothing,' I said disgustedly.

Well . . . not quite nothing. There was a jetty with groups of waiting men gathered upon it, and horse-drawn sleighs pulled up behind.

'Patience, Yanis,' said Dr Gomarus.

'But where is the town, doctor?'

'A little way inland, I believe. Don't worry, boy, these wild northern types don't live underground like trolls. And it is a village, not a town.'

I was not amused. Nor was my mood improved by the sight of so many boxes about our feet. Because Dr Gomarus claimed he needed to have his notes and equipment close by him until the very last minute, there had been no time to send them down to the baggage department for unloading, which meant we now had to carry them ourselves. The only piece of luggage that *had* gone, the doctor's battered old trunk of clothes.

I breathed out through my nose.

'Why is nothing happening?'

'Patience, Yanis,' the doctor said a second time. 'Besides there *is* something happening.'

I followed his eyes and saw a group of armed soldiers making its way down onto the frozen river. Ignoring the more straightforward routes— the ladder fixed to the jetty's side or the shallower reaches further off—the soldiers plunged through deep drifts of snow until finally reaching the ice, where they brushed snow crumbs off their great- coats, reformed lines, and began their march towards the ship. *Left-right, left-right* . . . I watched them, for it seemed everything else on board must first wait for them to be done with their business. They carried on marching right up to the ship, and still they marched on until I lost sight of them beneath the curve of the hull. I leaned out over the rail as far as I dared, seeing nothing but hearing voices barking sharp commands. Then abruptly the soldiers came back into view. *Left-right, left-right* . . . shoulders back, arms swinging as they marched towards the shore—and this time their number was increased by seven or eight dirty, unshaven prisoners, their hands in irons and feet shuffling beneath the weight of heavy chains.

'But . . . who are those men?'

Dr Gomarus frowned.

'You know as well as I. They are enemies of the Tsar.'

'Convicts, you mean? Going to prison?'

He didn't answer, and as I turned back to watch, I saw one of the men suddenly break free.

'*Oh look*, doctor, one's trying to escape—the one in the dirty blue coat—' My fingers remembered the touch of wool and cashmere, and the image of a terrified young man flashed into my head. 'But isn't that—'

'*That is nobody we know*, Yanis,' said Dr Gomarus sharply. 'We have never seen him before. *Ever*. You understand?'

I nodded my head reluctantly, noticing how the doctor pulled his coat more tightly about him in order to hide the splashes of dried red paint.

Down below us the escape attempt quickly came to nothing. The prisoner fell over his own chains before he had gone a dozen steps. In an instant an expressionless guard stood over him, the butt of his rifle raised, ready to beat him if he did not get to his feet and rejoin the others.

Somehow the young man found the strength to crawl his way back up and the mournful band continued on its way.

Watching the prisoners scramble clumsily up the deep banks of snow, I realized that steerage had not been the lowest and meanest deck on board ship, and that for all its white and gold paint and crisp-jacketed stewards, the *Ursus* contained some dark secrets.

When the prisoners had finally gone from sight, it was as if a black cloud had lifted: now unpleasantness could be put out of mind and ordinary life continue.

Sailors appeared on deck and in an almost carefree way strolled about their duties in the bright Arctic sunshine; and a young petty officer in a white uniform came across and saluted us.

'Sorry, gentlemen, you must go down into steerage if you wish to disembark. The gangway reaches no higher.'

'Does everyone?' I asked. 'What about passengers on First?'

He smiled indulgently.

'There are very few first-class passengers who came to Osva, sir. Very few indeed.'

I was thinking of just one—the Countess.

'Come on, Yanis,' said Dr Gomarus. 'Thank you, officer, we know the way.'

But first there was the small matter of the boxes . . . The doctor loaded me up like a donkey, a box in each hand, one on my back, and others hanging by straps from my shoulders. This left him with the camera, the box of skulls, and the small leather bag. I said nothing about the unfairness of the arrangement, but there must have been a hint of complaint in the way I looked at him.

'Ah, but think, Yanis, how much better this is than scrubbing other people's dirty washing.'

I opened my mouth to correct him—I had never in all my life scrubbed so much as a sock; I was the boy who sorted, the genius at recognizing stains, a . . . But I closed my mouth again. Dr Gomarus was perfectly right.

For once all doors into steerage were unlocked and thrown open. We went down into it. The vast echoey space was deserted except for a few crewmen sweeping up piles of stinking straw; the fires in the ovens burning low. We made for the hull doors which flooded the deck with unaccustomed daylight, finding the gangway there no more than a rickety ramp. At the bottom we stepped off onto the iron-hard river, and turning back, I blinked in wonder at the monumental runners that had carried us so smoothly over countless miles of ice, while being no less astonished at the great sweep of ship that seemed to hover over us, weightless in the air, like one of those stately white clouds you see in a blue summer sky.

As ever, Dr Gomarus was of a more practical frame of mind.

'I say, you there—'

He called to one of the local men stacking up crates as they were winched down from the cargo bay. The man came over, removing his leather gloves.

'Yes, sir?'

'My assistant and I are going to Osva.'

'Is that so, sir? But isn't everyone who gets off here?'

'We are staying with a Mrs Kropotkin at the manor house. Would you happen to know where that is?'

'Indeed I would, sir. Just follow the lane until the first set of walls and that'll be it; I'd say twenty minutes by foot or five in a sleigh.'

'Is it safe to walk?'

The old-timer grinned.

'That depends, sir—from wolves or revolutionaries?'

'Both, I should imagine.'

'Have no fear on either count, good sir, us folk in Osva like our wolves toothless and our revolutionaries safely tucked up in prison. Put your luggage down here if you like, sir, these crates are going up to Mrs Kropotkin's too. Seems some fine countess has been sent into exile, and of course she must take all her fineries with her.'

Hearing this was like being pricked awake.

'*Countess*, you say?'

The old fellow nodded. 'And I wouldn't be much surprised if that wasn't her right now.'

I spun round, clumsily knocking the boxes together, paying no heed to Dr Gomarus's tuts and sighs.

The Countess was just stepping off the ramp, stretching out her foot to the ice like a bather testing the water. She was swathed in flowing sable, a simple hat to match. Miss Mirsky followed her off and then led the Countess across to a waiting sleigh, gripping her elbow in that needlessly humiliating way of hers, her silver watch bouncing on her chest.

'Well,' said the old stevedore, nodding towards the Countess as she mounted the sleigh, then grinning and winking at us. 'That's one lady who wasn't sent into exile on account of her looks—*Ow!* Watch it, sonny.'

'Sorry,' I said picking up the box from his foot.
'I didn't notice you there.'

Unhindered by baggage, we managed a pleasant
stroll up the narrow lane to Mrs Kropotkin's.
Beyond the lane there was little we could see, for
on either side steep snowy banks rose up, and the
snow-heavy trees planted on top reached out to
form a continuous shadowy vault. It appeared
quite solid, but whenever the breeze stirred the
branches, trails of powdery flakes came trickling
down on us like rotten ceiling plaster. Underfoot
freshly fallen snow crunched.

Dr Gomarus turned and peered at me quizzically
through his pink spectacles.

'Are you thinking?'

'Oh yes, sir, but nothing important.'

He smiled.

'You mean, nothing that *I* would find important.'

I fixed my gaze on my boots; the doctor's pre-
ciseness at times made me wary of him. Hearing
sleigh-bells, we stopped and stepped aside to let a
sleigh pass. The driver waved his thanks to us and
we continued walking.

'Dr Gomarus—'

'Yes?'

'That woman—I mean, lady—the countess on the ship . . . Do you know much about her?'

'I know there was much talk concerning her, but I never listen to gossip.'

'But you *do* know something, don't you?'

'Why do you ask?'

'She . . . she was kind to me. I don't believe anyone that kind can ever do a bad thing—well, not bad enough to be sent into exile. If anyone is wicked, it's that Mirsky woman who travels with her; I can believe anything of her.'

The doctor snorted.

'*Kind equals good—good equals kind.* Come come, what sort of childish reasoning is that, boy? Haven't you learned anything since you've been with me? It isn't even logical.'

'I couldn't say about that, sir. All I *can* say is that sometimes you just know about a person, the way an animal does—and animals are never wrong. A cat always knows the best lap to curl up in.'

'Ha!' The doctor positively hooted. 'Are you telling me you reach conclusions like a cat, Yanis? Is this why you were named after one? And where will this remarkable talent of yours end? Shall I soon expect to find you bringing home a mouse for my supper?'

My face darkened; I wished now I had never raised the matter.

We walked in silence for a while, then the doctor eased his pace. He sighed.

'She has been sent into exile for eighteen months. The form of her punishment is, she must remain the whole time in a garrison town and be at least five hundred miles away from the Tsar's nearest palace.'

I forgot my sulk.

'Why? What did she do?'

'She incurred the displeasure of the Tsar.'

'The Countess? How?'

At this point the doctor stopped and blew his nose with a loud trumpeting sound, then fussed with his handkerchief, rubbing his nostrils until they were red.

'*Well?*' I said impatiently.

He looked at me, blandly.

'She refused to show him the proper amount of respect which, of course, is his accepted birthright . . . She refused to stand up for him when he entered a room.'

'And?'

'*And* that is it.'

I grabbed his sleeve.

'I don't understand. Just for that the Tsar sent her into exile for over a year?'

'That, my dear Yanis, is the penalty you pay when you cross a tsar.'

The manor house at Osva was a deep eaved, deep roofed wooden building with four stone chimneys. Plain but welcoming, its shutters pierced with heart-shaped holes, and over the main entrance a set of antlers. The stable block was set further back amongst the trees, and the snowy garden was surrounded by a high stockade lacking a gate at the gateway.

Dr Gomarus pulled the bell-pull and we heard a thin silvery sound far off inside. A moment or two later, feet came shuffling up the hallway.

The doctor removed his hat and smoothed down his hair. The door opened. A maid—a large awkward country girl—stood before us. She did not utter a word but stared open-mouthed at Dr Gomarus, then burst out laughing in our faces. Turning her head she bellowed back into the building, 'Mrs Kropotkin—Mrs Kropotkin, I got two more of 'em out here on the doorstep, one's a queer one with eyes like a rabbit's!'

We heard Mrs Kropotkin's voice as she approached.

'*Tonya*, what have I told you about being more courteous? Honestly, child, I despair.'

The door opened fully and a lady who I guessed must be Mrs Kropotkin was revealed taking charge of the situation.

'Ah . . . you must be Dr Gomarus . . . and this must be your son. Do come in. You are most welcome.'

Dr Gomarus, however, was going nowhere until he cleared up one small point.

'Not my son—*my boy*, madam. Yanis is my boy.'

'No matter, you are both no less welcome. Do come in out of the dreadful cold. Tonya—see about some tea, I'm sure Dr Gomarus would be glad of a nice cup.'

The maid sloped off back along the passage.

'And Tonya, dear, do make more of an effort to pick up your feet.'

Tonya's mutterings were dark and inaudible.

We went in, stamping our boots free of snow; Mrs Kropotkin extended her hand.

'So pleased to meet you, Dr Gomarus. You sounded such a nice young man in your letter. And now I can see for myself that you are.'

I smiled to myself, wondering how it was that Mrs Kropotkin managed to notice anything beyond the string of pearls around her neck. She was a hunchback, you see, and all her words were addressed to the ground.

They shook hands and she led us further into the house. Before we had time to take in much more than the dark panelling and black and white tiles on the floor, she pulled Dr Gomarus closer to her as if deciding to share a great secret with him. 'Of course,' she breathed, 'you were lucky that I could put you up at all. Do you know that I have a countess and a German prince staying here already? Yes, under this very roof. And now you—*a doctor*. Such an honour to be living among such nice people. Such an honour.'

As we reached a turn in the dimly lit passageway, I became aware of Miss Mirsky's angry voice, and coming round the corner, we found our way half-blocked by heavy, dark furniture, which was being removed from one of the rooms by two workmen. Both acted deaf to Miss Mirsky's bullying tones, one man even grinning at me then raising his eyebrows as if to say, 'Lord, doesn't she go on.'

Realizing she was getting nowhere with the men and seeing Mrs Kropotkin conveniently appear, Miss Mirsky turned her annoyance full on her.

'Mrs Kropotkin, you were informed that the Countess was bringing her own furniture. You were specifically notified of this. So why weren't these rooms made ready days ago?'

Mrs Kropotkin spoke quietly to the floor. 'Dear, yes, I suppose they could have been. But then what would I have had to sit my old bones on? This is, after all, Miss Mirsky, my home.'

Her words were pleasant to avoid any offence, but Miss Mirsky snorted, glared at the watch on her chest as if some vital timetable was thrown out of kilter and, turning on her heels, marched off. She had stared straight through the doctor and me: if she recognized us from the ship, she did not show it.

The man who had grinned said, 'City folk—city ways, always want tomorrow's work today . . . Where shall we put your furniture, missus?'

'Dear . . . The stables it shall have to be. I only hope the mice don't see fit to chew it.'

Mrs Kropotkin then took us upstairs to show Dr Gomarus his rooms. A camp bed had been set up for him in the library, with a small dressing room beyond.

'I'm afraid that the Countess and Prince have taken over my best rooms,' she said apologetically.

But Dr Gomarus was genuinely delighted to be in the company of so many books. 'Do you read?' he asked Mrs Kropotkin as he slowly wandered along the shelves.

'Oh, no-no-no, only silly romances, I'm afraid. These are my husband's books—not that he reads much these days. Poor man—he suffers so. Hardly gets up from his bed. I tell you it's a morning's work for him to keep down a mashed banana. But you must read them. Please, read any you like, doctor. Now I'll show this young man to his room and see where that girl's got to with your tea.'

Mrs Kropotkin led me to some rickety servants' stairs. She lit a candle before ushering me up them and followed a few steps behind, rubbing my back and saying, 'You will be a good boy, won't you? You will be sure not to make too much noise and disturb poor Mr Kropotkin.'

I promised to be always on my best behaviour.

'Good boy, I'm sure you will.'

At the top of the stairs, I found I didn't have a proper room but a windowless space in the attic, with one or two sorry pieces of furniture. My bed was a mattress on the floor.

Gripping my wrist, Mrs Kropotkin skewed round her head to face me. She lowered her voice like she had before with Dr Gomarus, as if what she was about to tell me was for my ears only.

'You know, there have already been two manors on this spot before this one. *Two*. And do you know why neither is here today?'

I shook my head dumbly.

'Fire. They burnt down because someone was careless with a candle. So you do promise not to play with candles, don't you? It wouldn't be nice if you made poor Mr Kropotkin and me homeless. Do you see?'

'I see.'

'Good—good.' She patted my head. 'Now hurry down and tell your master that you have been made comfortable.' She sighed. 'And I'll see about that nice cup of tea.'

That night in my attic I found it impossible to sleep. The wind droned and the beams and slats creaked; I lay listening to them in the darkness.

Yet it was not these that kept me awake, but thoughts of the Countess. I kept asking myself why she should want to cross the Tsar in so deliberate a way. After all, it was such a little thing to ask—to stand for him, hardly more than a smile or a wave. And she must have guessed at the troubles it would bring . . . Exile . . . Eighteen months . . . To me it seemed a lifetime.

I had begun to doze and was already half dreaming. I imagined the scene. A grand gold and mirrored chamber, a great flight of steps at one end. Everyone talking politely—lords, ladies, generals—but keeping a watchful eye on the doors at the top of the stairs.

And then, mysteriously, as if under their own power, the doors open. Conversation immediately breaks off—the imperial family has appeared. The bearded Tsar, his beautiful wife, their twin daughters, and the small doted-upon Tsarevich; each one looking as if he or she had stepped out of the print at Mrs Tiverzin's boarding-house.

The conductor raises his baton. Music. *Our beloved country—our beloved Tsar.* The scrape of chairs as everyone rises. (Well, as we know, not quite everyone.) The Countess pale, staring ahead, one gloved hand gripping the other so as not to betray how much she trembles.

The Tsar, his family, stop. The music trails away. The Tsar, father of all his people, looks down at the lone seated figure. He never gets angry in public, never shows an unworthy emotion, but a vein pulses in his temple. The Tsarina notices and touches his arm. She gazes around smiling to reassure everyone, *there has been a misunderstanding.* Discreetly she nods at the conductor.

Baton. 'Gentlemen of the orchestra.' The strains of the anthem start up again.

The imperial family descend several more steps before the Tsar again notices that the Countess still has not risen, but sits hand-in-hand with herself, staring defiantly ahead.

(By this time I was dreaming properly and the dream took on a life of its own. *I watch as if through a distant window*.)

I see the thin sickly daughters plucking at their father's perfectly starched uniform. 'Send her to prison, Papa—send her to prison,' they demand. 'Let Dr Gomarus have her and keep her head in a box.' The young Tsarevich in his sailor suit begins to cry, and the noise wakes up all Mrs Pafnutkin's babies in the next-door room. Their wailing sends the Tsar into a fit of fury—only he isn't the Tsar any more but a bear dressed as a hunter. There is an overwhelming sense of something terrible about to happen as everyone except the Countess disappears. The bear-king lifts his rifle and points it at her. He takes aim and—

'No—please—no!'

I sat up in bed sweating, the dream as real to me still as the bad taste in my mouth, so much so that I continued to hate the Tsar, wanting nothing more than to have a gun of my own and to hunt him down and shoot him again and again and again . . .

Eventually I calmed down, surprised at myself. Surprised at how much hatred I had in me—and all for our beloved Tsar. Sick with worry I began to shake. Was this how revolutionaries began? Hating the Tsar in their dreams? And if it was, perhaps I had begun a transformation that was as irreversible as when a maggot turns into a fly. And if I *did* become a revolutionary, would I end up as one of those filthy shuffling figures going off to prison in chains?

Hurriedly lighting my candle, I flew across to the side-table and the flaking mirror that was propped up there. In its reflection I closely examined every inch of my face, sticking out my tongue as I had for the doctor at the orphanage, searching for any visible sign of change. But what exactly was I looking for? Tufts of hair growing from my ears? Wild staring eyes? What did I know? I had only seen one revolutionary close to before, and then just for a moment.

In the mirror, however, all there ever was to see was my own frightened face staring back at me.

I rubbed my throat.

'It was only a dream.'

Still unsure, I put my hands together and bowed my head.

'God bless the Tsar,

Keep him strong and in health—

And, God, please believe me that I wouldn't have it any other way.'

I was awoken next morning by Dr Gomarus, who, having discovered that the library stepladder reached his ceiling, was able to bang on the underside of my floor and call for me at close quarters.

'Rouse yourself, Yanis, time to get up.'

I opened my eyes to cold unrelieved darkness and, yawning, lit my candle, dressed, and went down to the library. The fire hadn't been made and ice had formed on the glass inside the windows. Dr Gomarus was laying out his shaving things.

'Ah, good morning, Yanis, I trust you slept well? We have a big day ahead of us.'

He sent me down to the kitchen for hot water. When I got there I came across the maid, Tonya, sitting on the table, scratching herself and swinging her fat legs. She slowly lifted her eyes and looked over at me, holding my gaze.

I raised my empty jug.

'Hot water? For the doctor.'

With the smallest of nods she indicated the kettle on the range.

I went across and filled the jug, and just as I

was putting down the kettle, Tonya crept up behind me and before I knew it she had flung her arms around me and lifted me off my feet.

'Do you want to wrestle with me? I'm as strong as any man. Stronger. I can break walnuts with my bare hands. And see that table over there? I can lift it above my head. Right up. No kidding. You want to see?'

Indignantly I fought her off and fled from the room, spilling water in my haste—and all the time looking about me in case the Countess should have witnessed this shameful episode.

I gave Dr Gomarus the jug. He peered inside.

'Did you lose some?'

He sounded mildly curious.

'There wasn't much; the maid—she'd taken it.' And to change the subject: 'Dr Gomarus, why don't you let *me* shave you? I am your boy, after all. And you never use a mirror, every morning you leave soapsuds in your ears.'

He laughed.

'Well, that's one duty Goshka Kulich never volunteered himself for, lazy object that he was. So you don't think I cut a fine enough figure for the ladies here?'

A little crossly I said, 'It isn't right. You get blood on your collar. People don't expect it from a man like you. Perhaps they think you've been in a fight.'

He laughed again, and taking off his spectacles, sat down and allowed me to spread a towel around him.

I went to work with soap and cut-throat razor. I didn't miss a whisker.

'There.'

He ran his hand along his jowl and beamed at me appreciatively.

'Very good, Yanis, nice and close.'

I held out my hand before his face.

'See for yourself how steady I am.'

'Most impressive. Not a single shake, and I thought . . .'

'What?'

'Well, I expected you to be a little jittery about our going to the prison today. After all, it wasn't so long ago that—'

'It wasn't so long ago that I was a stupid laundry boy who knew nothing. I told you before, doctor, I feel fine about going to the prison and seeing the prisoners there'—and I added forcibly—'*all* of them.'

It was Mrs Kropotkin who served us our breakfast, chin resting on her chest and bearing the plates at arm's length before her.

'I daren't trust that girl Tonya with my nice china. She's that much of a carthorse she can chip a plate simply by looking at it—but such a sweet gentle nature underneath.'

Dr Gomarus and I sat close together at a corner of the big table in the dining room. Nobody else was up and the house felt quiet and undisturbed. Mrs Kropotkin gave us toast, cheese, and soft-boiled eggs. And strong hot coffee. Lots of it. She kept the pot warm in front of the fire and was forever re-filling our cups, right to the brim.

She could never be still: she bustled about folding and refolding napkins, brushing crumbs off the tablecloth into her palm, and of course to-ing and fro-ing with the coffee pot. Then suddenly she paused, and because it was so novel, we both looked at her.

'Doctor, while I'm still mindful of it, I'm having a formal dinner here tomorrow for all my nice new guests. Nothing too special in the way of food, alas. But you will be there, won't you? Say you will. It'll be so nice if all my guests meet each other properly.'

Caught off-guard with his coffee cup half raised to his mouth, Dr Gomarus was reluctantly forced to agree.

'Splendid,' beamed Mrs Kropotkin, and noticing a few spilt grains of sugar, she gave a little anguished cry and hurried to remove them.

Towards the end of the meal, the doorbell rang and a moment or two later we heard Tonya bawl out.

'Mrs Kro-pot-kin, it's him from up at the prison.'

'*Really*, that girl . . .'

Tutting to herself, Mrs Kropotkin went away and re-appeared shortly after, apologizing for her maid to Colonel Zhuk the prison governor, a glum little man with a walrus moustache and tired eyes, who was more concerned with brushing the snow off his shoulders than listening to excuses about slapdash servants.

Dr Gomarus rose to shake his hand.

'First day, eh, Gomarus? Thought I'd call and make myself known to you. Take you around— ease you into the way of things.'

'Most kind. If you'll excuse me a moment I'll just go and get our papers. You'll see everything is in order.'

Colonel Zhuk held up his hand, indicating not to bother, and sat down at the table.

'If you've got this far upriver I'm sure you must have had them checked and stamped at least a dozen times already. Besides, I'm sick to my back teeth of endlessly pushing paperwork about; it's not how I imagined I'd serve my country . . . Why, that would be most civil of you, Mrs Kropotkin—two sugars, if I may.'

Mrs Kropotkin was only too happy to fetch the coffee pot from the fireside, holding the handle with a cloth because it was so hot. She invited the colonel and his wife to her gathering the next day, and he accepted with about as much enthusiasm as Dr Gomarus had.

'Minus forty by the thermometer in my garden.' He absently stirred a spoon in his coffee.

'Fresh snow. About an inch. More to come, by the look of it.'

The colonel fell glumly silent after that, and even when we went out and climbed aboard his troika, he wordlessly leant forward to prod his driver in the back to get going. We set off down the carriageway. Under the sleigh's hood it was cold but dry, though the driver, who had sat waiting outside hunched over his reins, was covered in a thin dusting of snow, like ash.

Dr Gomarus attempted to strike up a conversation.

'You been governor here long, Colonel?'

'Two years, three months, and twelve days.'

Colonel Zhuk turned his weary eyes on us.

'Shall I tell you how I know so exactly? Each day I count it. I am so bored I have nothing else to do. Everyone counts out his time at Osva. I guarantee that by the end you will too. We are half off the map and there is nothing to do here except watch the clock, or each other, or the snow drifting down.'

'But don't the revolutionaries keep you on your toes?'

'God, how I wish they would. But I tell you, Gomarus, these revolutionary fellows are like bears, fierce and dangerous in the wild, but sad and pathetic once you get them behind bars. You'll see for yourself soon, here's the prison.'

I eagerly looked over the driver's shoulder, squinting my eyes at the flying snow and noticing how his front was caked in white. On one side of the road were the high prison walls, on the other the dreary log barracks of the garrison. In between, where the road ended, lay Osva, a disappointingly dreary village on the very edge of the forest and almost overwhelmed by snow, its church plain and whitewashed—the onion-shaped dome topping its belfry glimmering gold in the grey snow-flecked light.

The troika turned left into the prison, which was four storeys high and built around a court-yard, solid doors and barred windows facing inwards. Wind blew snow off the roof in a sudden swirling cloud, like smoke, and when the troika stopped, Colonel Zhuk quickly ushered Dr Gomarus into an office, leaving me to struggle behind, loaded down with the doctor's equipment. Colonel Zhuk was at an opened filing cabinet when I at last made it inside.

'I'll get you your permits so you can come and go whenever you like. If I were you I'd take this chance to warm yourselves at the stove, it's devil-ishly cold in the cells.'

Leaving behind a trail of wet footprints, Dr Gomarus and I padded across and stood before the metal stove: its smoke stack glowed red and several days' worth of old wood ash had been left piled up against its door. The clerks glanced up at us from their desks. None very busy. One played with his nib, another ate a bread roll, drop-ping crumbs down the front of his uniform. The tick of the wall clock was loud and lugubrious.

'Here we are.'

Colonel Zhuk came over, blowing on his wet signature.

'Captain Dudorov will take care of you. Dudorov, take the doctor and his assistant to block Two E, I've already sent word ahead—they're expecting you.'

Dudorov rose wearily and put on his greatcoat, slowly doing up every button right to his chin, then he led us back out into the court-yard. The sleigh was gone, as were its tracks. Clusters of snow made of two, three, or more conjoined flakes fell heavily from the sky. When Dudorov spoke, his voice came from inside his collar.

'This way.'

We struggled through knee-deep drifts; then Dr Gomarus stopped and gazed about him wonderingly.

'Why is it so quiet, Captain?'

Dudorov looked at him as if his question was a stupid one.

'Most prisoners have been sent out into the forest on logging duty. They work every day whatever the weather; the garrison sends a detachment to watch over them.'

'But never the prisoners from block Two E?'

'No. It isn't considered wise to let them outside the prison confines. They are the revolutionary leaders. They are the ones of most interest to you, are they not?'

Dr Gomarus began to move again, pulling his foot out of a snow-pile.

'They are indeed, and for good reason. The others are just foot soldiers, often driven to desperate acts by nothing more than hunger; so scientifically speaking they are of no use to me. The others—the gentlemen of block Two E—ahh, they are an entirely different matter. They choose to be revolutionaries out of a passionate belief in their cause. Do you see the difference?'

Captain Dudorov didn't answer; he looked bored. He took us through a door, up some stairs, and through another door leading onto a long corridor, one side of which was lined with barred cells. The two guards on duty immediately found their feet and saluted.

Captain Dudorov returned the salute in a lazy oh-well-if-I-have-to kind of fashion, then saluted us.

'I'll leave you here, doctor. These men will assist you in every way they can.'

And he turned and left, glad to get us off his hands.

The two guards hovered over us like servants anxious to please. I realized at once they were father and son, for in looks each was like a younger or older version of the other. With childlike curiosity they watched Dr Gomarus unload the boxes.

He paid them scant attention.

'We'll set up the camera first, Yanis. When I have taken enough plates, you can return to the manor and start work developing photographs ready for when I return.'

'Photographs?' said the younger guard, deeply impressed. He caught his father's eye and with winks and nods urged him to speak, which the older man did after several hesitant starts.

'Begging your pardon, your honour, this may appear a terrible imposition, but could you see your way to taking *our* photograph: one of us on either side of our most famous prisoner up there in the end cell? If I had such a photograph I would keep it on me always, and I'd show it to my grandchildren when I reached a great age.'

Dr Gomarus shook his head.

'Sorry, the camera is for scientific purposes only, not snapshots. Besides, which prisoner is so special that you would want to be photographed with him?'

'Why, Nikolay Kolchak, of course, your honour.'

Dr Gomarus deliberately kept his head low.

'Sorry. The answer is still no.'

Showing not the slightest disappointment or resentment, the young guard said, 'You must have read about Nikolay Kolchak? He's been in all the newspapers; he's the one who led a regiment of revolutionaries in the Koytava region and caused the Tsar all manner of grief there. Blowing up railway lines, cutting telegraph wires, and sabotaging oil pipes.'

'Not to mention the banks he robbed,' added the senior man with a wheezy laugh. 'Or the bombs he planted at a dozen or so main post offices.'

'A right holy terror,' agreed his son nodding and grinning as if in approval. 'The Tsar was forced to send a company of Black Rifles to hunt him down, and even then it took nearly a year to corner him.'

Dr Gomarus gave no sign of listening, he was busily assembling his camera, so the two guards turned their attention on me.

'And you know about the black skull, of course?'

'The black skull?'

I must have looked curious, as indeed I was.

'The black skull painted above his cell. It's the mark of a condemned man. If the Tsar refuses to pardon him, we must paint the skull red, then build a gallows and hang him.'

Sorrowfully the older guard shook his head.

'And what a sad day that will be. Such a natural gentleman, manners and everything. You would think such a one would be more inclined to serve our Tsar than fight against him.'

'It's true,' said the younger one. 'But when all is called to account we still have to remember his crimes against his majesty. *Long live the Tsar!*'

'Long live . . .' I began, at which point, like a pair of magpies, the two guards were diverted by the light of the paraffin wall lamps reflecting off the camera's brass lens tube, and immediately they were down on their knees beside Dr Gomarus, firing off half a dozen questions about what this did or how that worked.

I was left to wonder at what they had told me. About Nikolay Kolchak. Naturally I was intrigued, who wouldn't be? So it turned out he wasn't a double-headed fire-breathing devil after all. Now he was a *natural gentleman*—now he had *charm*, and he certainly seemed to have used it on the two guards.

I decided to try to catch a glimpse of him: just saunter up and glance casually into his cell, the one at the end they had said. If need be I could pretend I was looking for someone else.

So I crept away from Dr Gomarus, who was patiently explaining elementary photography, and approached the last cell. Lifting my eyes I saw with a delicious thrill of horror the black skull— but my horror turned real enough the moment I lowered them again, for I found myself meeting the steady gaze of Nikolay Kolchak; his eyes intensely blue.

'Good morning. Were you hoping to catch the monkey before they dangle him on a string?'

I stopped dead in my tracks like someone caught stealing. I kept looking away then looking back again, unable to believe how very ordinary he was. He wouldn't stand out in a crowd. No ... that wasn't true. With his blond hair and handsome looks, Nikolay Kolchak would stand out well enough.

He lay on his bunk, one hand behind his head and the book he had been reading lying flat against his chest; in his other hand he held a pair of pince-nez spectacles. He wore several coats, a balaclava, scarf, and a pair of fingerless mittens. The mittens were made out of old socks and the balaclava was pushed back behind his ears.

He beckoned me closer and when I did not move, he said, 'Don't worry, I'm a revolutionary not a leper. You won't catch anything from me— least of all my nasty revolutionary ideas.'

He spoke with a wry smile as if everything amused him.

Awkwardly I shuffled a pace or two forward.

'What do they call you?'

I decided it wouldn't hurt to tell him, even though he was an enemy of the Tsar.

'Yanis,' I whispered.

'Yanis, eh? And are you with that scientist fellow?'

I nodded.

'And what is his name again?'

'Dr Gomarus.'

'Dr Gomarus . . . Are you his servant?'

'I'm his assistant.'

Nikolay Kolchak smiled as I proudly clung to my title.

'Of course, *assistant*. Well, Dr Gomarus's assistant, I hear you have come a thousand miles to measure my head. I hear your Dr Gomarus can prove I'm a wild lawless revolutionary because of the length of my nose—or is it the curl of my eyelashes?'

'Oh, it's much more complicated than that—'

I stopped short, realizing I had no idea how much more complicated.

He smiled. 'I hope so . . .'

Putting down his book, he climbed off his bunk and crossed over to the cell door, leaning against the bars, his arms folded. I flinched but did not move away. Despite his friendly manner I had no cause to trust him and—I'll freely admit it now—I was still much afraid of his reputation.

'Tell me, Yanis, when did you arrive in Osva?'

'Yesterday. Aboard the *Ursus*. We are staying at the manor—at Mrs Kropotkin's place.'

He nodded and looked thoughtful as if this was no more than he expected.

Just then the young guard came up, whistling, and I moved aside for him to unlock the door.

'They're coming to take your photograph, sir. What do you say to that?'

Nikolay Kolchak smiled his easy smile.

'I say I hope they make me look as handsome as those pictures of actors you see outside theatres.'

The guard chuckled to himself as he arranged a stool for him, giving the seat an extra shine with his cuff before Nikolay Kolchak sat down on it. He was in place and waiting when Dr Gomarus and the older guard arrived; Dr Gomarus with the camera and tripod slung over his shoulder.

He was brisk and businesslike.

'I require two photographic images of you. One from the front—one in profile. And please, no smiling. Then I shall take a few straightforward measurements. That's all. There's nothing that will hurt you or cause you distress in any way.'

'*Nothing*, dear doctor? I assure you it will pain me a great deal not to smile and have to be at my glummest for you.'

The guards looked at each other and chuckled affectionately. I wondered if they were as fond of the other prisoners. Somehow I doubted it.

Nikolay Kolchak sat patiently for his photographs, holding a slate with his name and number on it; and he was not a little amused when

Dr Gomarus began measuring his head with those murderous-looking callipers of his. After his head, his eyes, ears, nose, and mouth were measured in detail, as were the angles and distances between them. Dr Gomarus jotted down notes on everything, recording the bumps and ridges on his skull, the precise colour of his eyes (blue G7-III from the glass match), and the shape, size, and angles of various other features.

When the doctor was finally done, Nikolay Kolchak stood and shook him by the hand.

'I hope my old brainbox has proved diverting and worth your long journey, doctor.'

'In time I shall see.'

'Thank you, Mr Kolchak,' said the younger guard after we had all trooped out and he was turning the key in the lock.

Nikolay Kolchak settled back down on his bunk.

'Anything to help the cause of my fellow man.'

Dr Gomarus and the two guards moved on to the next prisoner, but I hesitated, almost as if waiting for Nikolay Kolchak to dismiss me. For no longer was I frightened of him; if anything I had begun to like him. And I half hoped he liked me.

'Shall I go?' I asked.

'If you want to . . . although I would much prefer it if you stayed. Books help pass the time, but having a visitor of one's own is rather special.'

So I stayed and we began to talk—or rather he did, I simply listened to the tales that spilled out of him. Tales from the days he roamed as wild as a wolf; and although he and his men must have been blowing up post offices and cutting telegraph wires at the time, he never mentioned these things. Instead he told me about how he had nearly lost his life trapped on an ice-floe; and how he was once so hungry he had fought a bear over a walrus carcass; and how he had lived amongst the Koy people as one of their own, driving his own team of pure white huskies, a privilege usually only allowed to a prince of the tribe.

'To speak of these adventures now,' he said smiling sadly, 'is like talking about another man's life. Yanis, will you do something for me?'

'What?'

'You have an honest face; I trust you and I need some things. Will you take my silver pocket watch and sell it for me? That will raise the money. You see I'm desperately in need of soap and thick cotton vests. I haven't changed my clothes once since I got here and quite frankly I'm beginning to get sick of smelling like a mangy old bear. But there are other things too; if you want I could write you a list.'

'I don't know...'

'Everyone does it. It's not breaking any rule, only the other prisoners have family and people they trust to bring them the extras they need.'

'What about the guards? Won't they help you?'

He shook his head.

'They are good to me in their own way but they wouldn't do this. It might be seen as a bribe. But they wouldn't stop anyone else. I'm told there's a woman in the village who makes a living out of buying from prisoners. She lives in the green house opposite the church. But it needs someone who will go there.'

He held out his watch.

'What harm is there in it?'

None that I saw, but still I looked round guiltily as I took the watch.

'Press for at least a hundred draculs. Tell her, through blizzards and driving rain it's never once let me down.'

Having got me to take it, he hurried over and sat on his bed, and ripping the endpaper from the book he had been reading, began composing his list.

'Vests . . . soap . . . more writing paper, as you can see—and pencils, I need more pencils to write with . . . Tobacco . . . matches . . . and one small bottle of iodine. There, that should be enough for the time being.'

He came back and brandished the list at me.

I hesitated in taking it.

'What's wrong now?'

'Nothing, it's only . . . *I can't read.*'

It was a humiliating confession to have to make. But he smiled encouragingly.

'Then all you have to do is present the list. Simple.'

'I suppose.'

'Here, take it.'

I took it and slowly folded it up.

'I'll see what I can do.'

'Yanis, you're a true friend.'

When Dr Gomarus was finally ready, he called for me and handed me a small airtight box containing eight newly taken plates, then sent me off to Mrs Kropotkin's to develop them.

'And no snow-balling on the way.'

'*Doctor,*' I said, affronted, 'I'm not a baby, I'm your assistant.'

Even so, instead of going straight to the manor, I found myself knocking at the door of the shabby green house opposite the church.

It opened a crack.

A suspicious voice spoke out of the gloom.

'What do you want? I'm a poor woman. There's nothing here for you.'

'I . . . I've come to sell something.'

After a pause, the door opened a little more to reveal a filthy old woman, her face tightly bound in a headscarf. She wore several shawls and both these and her dress were covered in cat hairs. I tried to hold my breath. The powerful stink of cat came wafting out on a draught of over-heated air, and several of the yowling creatures rubbed themselves against the old woman's ankles, vying for her attention.

'You have, dearie? Quickly, let me see.'

Her sly peasant eyes gleamed.

I showed her the watch and reluctantly let her hold it to examine it more closely. Expertly she turned it over in her filthy fingers, the cats all the time crying around her. The watch chimed delicately.

'Fifty-five draculs.'

'But . . . it's a good watch.'

'That's as maybe, dearie, but it's engraved. Who wants a watch with someone else's initials on it? Fifty-five. It's a fair price. Take it or go on your way.'

Cursing her under my breath, I accepted and ran all the way to the government store, the brightest lit building in the village. There I bought what I could.

It was only when I was outside again that I realized the soap was the same sort that was used on collars and cuffs at the orphanage, with the familiar unsmiling portrait of the Tsar on the box, and whose well-known slogan Mrs Pafnutkin used to bellow like a war cry whenever we grew slack.

Cleanse with the strength of the Tsar.

I only hoped Nikolay Kolchak would appreciate the joke.

Having done this much for a prisoner I had only known for a few hours, I now hurried down the lane guiltily aware that I had neglected Dr Gomarus's work for long enough. Reaching the enclosed garden, I marched up to the manor and yanked on the bell-pull, my expression deliberately set hard to show that pest Tonya what I really thought of her. The door opened immediately and my expression dissolved into confusion. It was the Countess.

She smiled and I was suddenly conscious that I was made up of every awkward part a body could be made from. I didn't know what to say: I imagined in her eyes this made me look hopelessly clumsy or stupid, and I blushed—my misery complete. Even so I managed to take in every detail of her—the plain, grey dress made of softest wool, the white collar and cuffs. Over her dress she wore a simple apron as if she were nothing more than a lowly servant—yet one a million miles removed from that clodhopper Tonya.

'Ah, Yanis, my little friend from the *Ursus*; Mrs Kropotkin has been telling me all about you. Well well, how impressive—a scientist, no less. Who would believe it? I'm not sure I've met a scientist in my whole life before, and I have to say I'm intrigued.'

Somehow I managed to get into the hallway and remove my cap. I was aware she was gazing at me, smiling, waiting for me to speak.

'Not a scientist, Countess.'

'Sorry?'

'Me . . . I'm not . . . not one—a scientist. Dr Gomarus, he's the scientist . . . I'm just his assistant.'

She was so beautiful it made me nervous.

I heard her gentle laugh.

'I'm sure you are much cleverer than that, and I would so love to know more about you and what you do.'

155

'Me, Countess? You want to know more about me?'

A blush rose again, which the Countess couldn't fail but notice.

'Forgive me, Yanis, how tactless of me; I see how it is and I have embarrassed you.'

'No . . .'

'Oh, but I have. Forget what I have just said, I had no right to ask. You have probably discovered why I have been sent here and think it less than proper that we should talk together in so casual a manner. I understand. People gossip and I am under a cloud; lost reputations are almost impossible to regain.'

Abruptly she turned to go.

'No—please, Countess. I didn't mean . . . We can talk if you like. I want to.'

I had no idea what I could talk to a countess about, but I saw her smooth invisible wrinkles from her apron before slowly turning back.

'Only if you are quite sure.'

I nodded enthusiastically and she touched my arm with the tips of her fingers.

'I'm so glad. I really want nothing more than for us to be friends. You see, it's hard, Yanis. I know I ought not to complain, but the ridiculous truth is I am not used to my own company. Nor the company of those who hold no interest for me. Mrs Kropotkin is such a treasure in many ways, but her conversation is so worthy; I swear she is desperate not to say something that might offend me, that is when she isn't charging off to clean up after her maid. And Miss Mirsky—well, Miss Mirsky and I do not have a great deal in common—certainly not military bands or the lives and works of lesser saints. Everyone else is either busy or away. The plain fact is, Yanis, I have no one I can talk to.' With a deep sigh she raised her brimming eyes to the ceiling. 'I shall grow dull during my stay in Osva. I shall lose my sparkle, I shall shrivel away into nothing . . . unless, that is, I can make one true and special friend.' She lowered her eyes to meet mine. 'All I'll ever ask is that you now and again spare me five minutes of your time.'

'Of course, Countess. Whenever you like.'

'Really?' She blinked away her tears and smiled. 'And you will not find it inconvenient or too odious a chore?'

'No—I should look forward to it very much.'

'Then you may yet be the saving of me, Yanis.'

She raised my chin with a crooked finger, her voice a murmur.

'How sweet you are, listening to my silly concerns when you have been working hard at the prison. Mrs Kropotkin says you've been there since early this morning. Can this be true?'

I nodded.

'Shall I tell you what I do there?'

She laughed.

'Anything, so long as it takes me out of these four dreary walls. But come warm yourself by the fire. You must be frozen, and I have kept you out here in the hall talking all this time.'

Unable to resist, I found myself leaving Nikolay Kolchak's supplies and Dr Gomarus's box of plates by the door and hurrying after her like a little dog.

We went through into her drawing room.

Hearing me gasp, she turned and smiled at me again.

'What do you think? Do you approve of my few precious pieces and the way I've arranged them?'

How could I not? I surveyed the room more slowly, seeing how it had been transformed by the Countess's elegant furniture, which flanked the fireplace and was carefully grouped around a matching pair of beautifully patterned carpets. The walls were hung with fine gilt mirrors and landscapes, while the Countess's smaller treasures were displayed on sideboards or inside glass cabinets—china figurines, silver candelabras, coloured crystal, painted bowls. Even the curtains belonged to her. They had to. Maroon plush trimmed with golden fringing did not suggest Mrs Kropotkin's heavy hand; and it was pure Countess the way they dramatically framed the windows. Like a stage; outside, the mounds of snow waiting for the actors to appear from the wings.

The Countess sat—no, rather she perched upon a sofa and gestured I should have the chair opposite. I made my way around the edges of a carpet so as not to leave the imprints of my boots, and sat where I had been shown.

The Countess smiled welcomingly.

'I could ring for the maid for some tea . . . ? That is, if she would come.'

I shook my head.

'Thank you . . . but no.' Briefly my eyes flickered around the room. 'Miss Mirsky? Isn't she with you today?'

'Ah, *dear* Miss Mirsky . . . no, she's asleep in her room. When there is nobody around to disturb me, she likes to take a nap; such a busy, diligent woman. It would be cruel of us to interrupt her, don't you agree?'

'Yes.'

I was as glad of her absence as the Countess pretended not to be, but even without Miss Mirsky I still felt awkward in the Countess's

159

presence, sitting straight-backed in that jewel-box of a room.

Self-consciously I made a small movement with my hand.

'It feels a little strange, Countess.'

'What does?'

'Being here in your room. It's so different after the prison.'

There was a pause in which the Countess might have added: but for me it is still a prison—yet instead she just smiled wistfully.

'Yes, go on, you were about to tell me all about it. You went there this morning with that clever Dr Gomarus. Is he studying a particular disease?'

'No, not really. He's only interested in heads. He likes to measure them.'

'*Gracious*. Like Madame Tourville when I go for a hat fitting?'

'Yes—*no*. I don't know, Countess. He compares them and takes notes. Lots of notes. That's all I know.'

The Countess nodded as if this made perfect sense.

'Mrs Kropotkin says you have all manner of strange equipment, each in its own special box. She says—*Oh*, but forgive me, perhaps I should not pry.'

'*No, no. It isn't a secret*, really it's not. It's what I do—I develop photographs of the prisoners.'

'The revolutionaries?'

'Yes . . . the important ones, at least.'

'Fascinating. And you get to meet them?'

I nodded.

'I have a pass, I can come and go as I please.'

'I expect the prisoners envy you that?'

Curiously, it was not something I had stopped to consider.

I shrugged.

'Yes,' I said. 'I expect they do.'

As I finished speaking a clock chimed three o'clock. I turned to the silvery sound. The clock was in the form of an egg on the back of a black elephant—comic—and a little out of place in that otherwise tasteful room.

The Countess pressed a hand to her throat.

'Such a silly frivolous thing, but it was a present from my dear old grandpapa on my sixteenth birthday.'

She looked hardly any older and so pretty as her cheeks coloured that suddenly I had an overwhelming desire to say something that might impress her or win her admiration.

A thought came into my head.

'An amazing thing happened to me at the prison today—I met the world famous Nikolay Kolchak.

161

He spoke to me! Not only that, he asked me to do him a favour. He said I have an honest face, he said he trusted me. Then he gave me his solid silver watch to sell because all he wanted were some vests and soap and a few other things—and I had to go into the village to sell it. I did my best for him—honest I did, but when I tried to get a fair price I was beaten down. And that didn't seem right somehow, for although he's a revolutionary all the guards admire him, and to cheat a man just before he's hung, well, somehow it didn't seem right—'

I noticed the Countess was staring straight ahead into the snowy garden, her expression one I could not read. *Idiot*—why did I have to ramble on so?

'Countess . . . ? If I have spoken too much or out of turn . . .'

Her hand was over her mouth, her eyes bright with tears. Then, almost as if remembering where she was, she turned to me, slowly regaining her composure.

'Forgive me, Yanis, I am a silly sentimental woman. But hearing your story . . . it touched me. That poor man reduced to selling his most precious treasure in order to make his wretched life more bearable. *Oh* . . .' She grew angry. 'I don't care who he is, condemned prisoner or revolutionary, he is still a man. And every man deserves some small measure of dignity, if only his watch.'

'He never once complained, Countess. The guards all say he's a gentleman.'

'Perhaps they do. But if they looked after him better there would be no need for him to sell his watch!'

She leapt up and paced the floor.

'It's monstrous how we treat each other. Wouldn't you agree, Yanis . . . ? See—see, we are of one mind on the matter. We should not behave as if everyone is our enemy. If each person were to help just one other, think what could be achieved in this world. But these are fine words, Yanis; we must act not talk.'

I kept nodding enthusiastically throughout her speech, but didn't really understand what she was talking about. Now I watched her cross to a small bureau, open a drawer, and take something out; when she returned I saw two crisp hundred dracul notes fanned out in her hand.

'Please, Yanis, take this money and run down to the village and rescue that poor man's watch. *Hurry*. If you're quick I'll give you five draculs as a reward.'

I jumped up and took the money, carried along by the moment.

'I'll get the watch, you'll see, but I'll not take a penny piece for it!'

The Countess lifted my hand and squeezed it, then rubbed my cheek with her knuckle.

'Dear sweet boy, see, once again you are my champion. And here, take my handkerchief so you can wrap the watch safely in it.'

As she handed it to me she kept her eyes lowered.

'One more thing, dear Yanis, you *will* be sure to keep this a matter just between you and me—our little secret? I wouldn't wish certain people to think me a great fool for parting so easily with my money.'

I guessed she meant Miss Mirsky and promised *on my life* not to betray her to anyone, and you know, at that moment I really meant it.

The floating feeling I had when I left the Countess lasted until I reached the village. Then I was quickly brought back to earth. I discovered that in the space of an hour Nikolay Kolchak's silver watch had risen sixty draculs. The greedy old witch in the green clapperboard house licked her lips whenever money was mentioned. Beyond this, she showed no interest in me or why I was so desperate to have the timepiece back again quite so soon after selling it. Indeed she acted as if I were an entirely different person.

She dangled the watch before my eyes and I was tempted to snatch it and run.

'Such a toothsome little object, all engraved,' she said accompanied by the ceaseless wail of her cats. 'One hundred and fifteen draculs. Take it or be on your way.'

And she licked her lips.

With the watch bought and making a comfortable weight in my pocket, I left the village; already the first lanterns were being lit, and darkness was creeping out of the forest, where it had lain curled up amongst the roots all day.

The dropping temperature made my skin prickle.

'Yanis—Yanis!'

Hearing the doctor call, I turned—he too was making his way home. He hurried to catch me up.

'What are you doing here, boy?'

'An errand for the Countess, doctor.'

'*What*, you have finished developing the photographs already?'

Guiltily I looked down.

'Sorry, Dr Gomarus . . . but I haven't managed to start that yet.'

'Nor will you today, boy—nor will you. It's too late now: you should have got that underway hours ago when you could have made full use of the daylight.'

'Sorry, sir, I'll get up first thing tomorrow and see they get done. I promise. Only the Countess—'

'The Countess must find others to do her running. Yanis, *I* am your master.'

His mouth twitched and I knew he was very angry.

'Yes, Dr Gomarus, I'll make sure it never happens again.'

Before blowing out my candle, I set Nikolay Kolchak's watch close by my mattress, its ticking loud in the darkness; but in the morning, when I lit the candle again, it showed me that it was four o'clock and time to get up.

It was bitterly cold out of bed; I blew into my hands to stop them from getting stiff and clumsy. For not only had I the eight original plates to develop but an additional four which the doctor had taken after I had left him at the prison.

Twelve plates meant a lot of work—with the promise of more to come.

Before starting, though, I drank down six raw egg yokes, which I had separated the previous day. Not that I was in any way fond of raw yokes—in fact I found them unpleasantly thick and tasteless—the point of the separating being to collect the whites, which were used in the developing process. But the orphan in me refused to waste good food. I swallowed down every last bit of yoke, including the little slivers of ice that had formed in the night, and set the empty cup down.

The nourishment seemed to bring me more out of my sleep and clear my head, which was good as I couldn't afford to make any mistakes— and it would be so easy to lose concentration.

You see, in creating a photograph there are two distinct parts, both complex. The first part is to prepare the glass plate from the camera; the second is to use that plate to make a print. As darkness is vital for much of the time, my windowless attic might have been made for the purpose. I set out everything I needed in the correct order, a stillness about me like a priest beginning his rites. I was ready. I covered the candle with its red protective shade and began.

From its special carrying box, I took out the first plate, wet and sticky with silver nitrate solution. I washed it with developer, and then water, and placed it in a bath of fixing-agent. I washed the plate again, holding it up to the shaded candle to examine the ghostly negative image upon it. It seemed good, no scratches. Now all I needed to do was warm the varnish over the flame and coat it. The plate was then done. After that I could do no more until the sun came up. As Dr Gomarus had pointed out so shortly the previous day, I needed natural light to produce a finished photograph and daybreak was hours away. Still, this gave me the opportunity to prepare the other plates, and putting aside the first one, I carefully took out the next, and so the business went on until a burst of knocking took me by surprise.

'*Breakfast, Yanis.*'

I went down with the doctor. I wasn't hungry, but Mrs Kropotkin's coffee was good—bitter and hot. I felt my heart quickening as I drank it. As for the doctor, he seemed to have forgiven me. I saw him studying my tired face and perhaps he guessed that I had been working hard to redeem myself. Or perhaps he had heard me creeping around above his room in the early hours.

He said, 'Finish your work off here, Yanis, before you join me at the prison. There is nothing you can do there in any case, not till I have photographed the next batch of prisoners, and these'll be ready when you arrive.'

'Yes, doctor, I'll be there just as quickly as I can.'

After I left him, I walked slowly back to the attic, on the way hoping to catch a glimpse of the Countess, but her rooms were silent, her doors firmly shut.

By ten o'clock I was ready to make a print. I'd prepared the paper beforehand by dipping it into a mixture of egg white and chloride, and now it was dry I put a sheet into the printing frame, carefully positioning the first glass negative over the top.

Exposure to daylight would do the rest.

So with the loaded printing frame held tightly beneath my arm, I made my way back down through the house and slipped out of a side door. The garden appeared deserted, but then from the wilderness area I heard the sound of voices. First a man's voice and then the softer briefer sound of a woman. The man was doing most of the talking, his tone boastful and full of self-importance, while the woman was called upon now and again to defer to him with a 'yes' or a 'no'. At once I recognized that second, gentler voice as belonging to the Countess and all my senses sprang alert.

As I waited, looking towards the spot from which the voices arose, the two speakers emerged from the trees, treading a path of cleared snow—the Countess swathed in grey fox fur, accompanied by a tall man with a waxed moustache, its ends pinched out into points. And then, silently, a few paces behind them, I saw the dour figure of Miss Mirsky—her presence like a dark cloud at a picnic—keeping in step with the company and determinedly following every word that was said.

The Countess was obviously bored. Her companion was so tall he had to stoop his head to be sure of her ear. The Countess did not look his way but stared fixedly ahead at the path, muttering her 'yes' or 'no' from time to time; for his conversation was limited to a single subject—*hunting*—and varied only in the type of animal he had slaughtered or the place or manner in which he had slaughtered it.

The printing frame and photograph forgotten, I watched them approach. At last, seeing me there, the Countess's face broke into a grateful smile.

'Oh, Yanis. *Good morning* to you.'

I nodded respectfully and the tall gentleman lifted his monocle and gave me a haughty stare.

'Yanis, my sweet boy, I have a sudden desire to know the time.'

With a flourish I could not resist (and before Miss Mirsky beat me with her own time-piece), I took out Nikolay Kolchak's silver watch and politely informed her it was quarter past ten.

She nodded and smiled back her secret approval.

'And who is this exactly?' demanded the man, his voice abrupt to the point of rudeness.

'This? Why this, sir, is my good friend Yanis, Dr Gomarus's assistant.'

'And what does he do? Impertinently lurk around empty gardens waiting for passers-by to ask him the time. Hmm? A talking sundial? If that is so, I say there is no better cure for an idle fellow than an hour's good graft in the stables. He can start by rubbing down my horse, after that there's always plenty of polishing needing to be done. Hmm?'

The Countess playfully tapped the man's hand.

'Now, now, I'm sure Dr Gomarus keeps the boy on his toes—besides, sir, you were saying . . . ? About that bear in Szegod.'

'Ah, yes . . .'

They moved off, Miss Mirsky glaring back at me, but I didn't care: I felt myself aglow with triumph. My timing (in all senses) had been perfect. But I couldn't say I liked the look of this new fellow, or his interest in the Countess, for I had seen the way he had stolen glances at her when he thought she didn't notice.

Determined to find out more, I raced to the kitchen and flew in through the door. Mrs Kropotkin's humpback was bent over the sink as she peeled potatoes, while Tonya sat on the draining board, her dress pulled up to her knees, regaling her with sensational stories.

'. . . And when they found the axe, they knew it was the right one—the one that had killed him, because there was blood all over it and his footprints led from the cellar—'

She broke off in surprise when I came rushing in (but brazenly did not roll down her dress, I noticed, so that her bare knees were in my full view all the time). Cumbersomely Mrs Kropotkin sidestepped round to see who was there, then smiled in recognition.

'That man—' I said in a breathless gasp, 'the one with the Countess in the garden. Who is he?'

'Ah, but of course, you won't have met him yet,' said Mrs Kropotkin turning and continuing with her peeling. 'That is my other special guest, my German Prince.'

'The German Prince . . . yes, yes I'd forgotten about him. But what is he doing here in Osva?'

'Hunting, of course, dear. That's all a prince ever does. Yet such a nice, generous man, always bringing meat home for the pot.'

'You should see his manservant Kazan,' put in Tonya pulling a face. 'A Tabrezian with eyes black as coals. And he doesn't speak. His tongue was cut out by the enemy after the Battle of the Goats in the Finlandian Wars.'

'*Tonya!*'

Mrs Kropotkin pretended to be shocked.

'You shouldn't go saying such things, it's pure gossip.'

'But it's true, Mrs Kropotkin, everyone knows it, and I'll tell you what else is true. The Prince, he's got a proper soft spot for the Countess. He's always trying to catch her eye, you must have noticed? You don't think . . . *no* . . . but what if they fell for each other and decided to get married?'

I glared at her savagely, suddenly consumed by an uncontrollable fury.

'Shut up! Just be quiet, why don't you! You could drive a person mad with your stupid, brainless talk. Besides, it's nothing to do with you *what* the Countess does!'

And as I fled from the kitchen, Tonya's baffled laughter followed me up the stairs.

Safe back in the darkness of my attic, I grew more and more ashamed at my outburst as my temper cooled. What was I thinking of? Why shouldn't the Countess marry a German prince if she wanted to? What did it matter to me? I tried to pace the floor, but after bumping my head a few times I gloomily sat down and wondered what to do. I refused to go anywhere near the kitchen— *oh no*—my sense of embarrassment was too great for that, but neither did I feel it right I should let down Dr Gomarus, who was depending on me and had given me a second chance.

Then I had an idea—and to my relief it worked.

I found that by leaning from the best-positioned of the library windows, I had all the daylight I needed. I could print a perfect picture. Below me lay the empty garden. I tried not to look at it. It reminded me of how my glorious moment with the Countess had been spoilt.

By one o'clock I was finished, and I slunk out of the house like a whipped dog, relieved not to meet anyone on the way. I trudged towards the village, the sun now so brilliant that the snow dazzled me.

Distantly I heard a sergeant barking out orders.

On their parade ground soldiers were being drilled. That is, some were being drilled while others cleared away the snow to make the parade ground bigger. Then they swapped over, shovels being exchanged for rifles.

I didn't stop to watch but made directly for the prison. Inside, it struck me no less grim than before: the bright sunlight never quite penetrating the shadow of its high walls. I crossed the courtyard and entered the building, and there stumbled at once upon three guards openly drinking vodka on the stairs. They did not ask who I was or to see my papers, but merely lowered their voices until I was safely out of earshot. I hurried on—not immediately to find Dr Gomarus, however, but making my way instead to Nikolay Kolchak's cell.

I came upon him lying on his bed smoking a briar-root pipe. He jumped up the moment I appeared. Feeling suddenly awkward and shy, I thrust the package of supplies at him without a word. Not noticing my lack of manners, he laughed out in delight.

'Well—well.'

He shook the package, pretending to guess what was inside.

'It's just like Christmas,' he said, and he shouted down to the older guard. 'I said it's just like Christmas up here.'

The guard grinned good-naturedly.

'I hope that boy hasn't smuggled you a gun.'

'Oh, but he has,' said Nikolay Kolchak. 'And twenty rounds of ammunition and a master key to every door, so you better watch out.'

The guard laughed.

'That's a good one.'

Rolling his eyes, Nikolay Kolchak turned back to me.

'And I've something else,' I said stumblingly. 'I—I did this. An extra copy—just don't tell Dr Gomarus. He doesn't approve of snapshots.'

I handed him the very first photograph the doctor had taken of him the previous day.

Nikolay Kolchak took it and studied it closely, his smile bursting into a laugh.

'But your doctor promised he would make me look handsome . . . oh, but I suppose it might do on a wanted poster.' He held it up to his face. 'What do you think? *Reward: Ten thousand draculs. Dead or Alive.*'

However, I knew despite his joking he was pleased with it, and this gave me as much pleasure as anticipating what was to come next.

I dipped my fingers into my pocket.

'I've saved the best till last. Hold out your hand.'

He obliged me and I dropped the little wrapped bundle into it.

'What's this—feels familiar?'

'See for yourself.'

He began undoing the knot in the handkerchief but stopped when he noticed the embroidery on it.

'Yanis . . . this is not a boy's handkerchief.'

'No, it belongs to a lady at the manor. A countess. I told her all about you and she was moved to tears that you had to sell your watch, so she bought it back and asked me to give it to you. Please don't think it charity and return it! I know she's a stranger to you, but if ever you met her you'd understand just how good and fine a person she really is.'

'I believe she must be. You must tell her—*no*, I have a better idea.' He took his photograph, wrote something on the back and held it out to me.

'Will you give her this?'

I nodded.

He glanced to both sides, gripping the bars so tightly that his knuckles were white.

'But you must keep it a secret.'

'I've already promised the Countess that, and I would not dream of betraying such a lady.'

'Good boy.'

He suddenly relaxed, pressing his forehead against the metal bars.

'I'd better go now . . . Dr Gomarus . . . He'll be wondering . . .'

'Yes, you run along, Yanis. You mustn't keep your master waiting. *And thank you.*'

Dr Gomarus peered up at me over the top of his pink spectacles.

'Ah, Yanis, a timely appearance, I have another eight plates ready for you.'

And with little more said, I found myself leaving the prison and making my way back down the lane, following my own back-to-front footprints.

The footprints eventually stopped where they had begun, at the manor's front door, and there I hesitated, wondering who would come and let me in. A smirking Tonya? Or an overly sympathetic Mrs Kropotkin? Either way I dreaded it. But I didn't need to concern myself. In the end it was the Countess who answered the bell, and so quickly, it was almost as if she had been listening out for me.

Furtively she glanced over her shoulder.

'*Dear* Miss Mirsky has just popped into her room for her embroidery.'

She was warning me we hadn't much time.

Quickly I handed her the money I owed her from the previous day—

'Nikolay Kolchak was extremely grateful for your concern, Countess.'

—and then I gave her the photograph.

She must have been surprised at how handsome he was, for I heard her gasp.

'He's written a note to you on the back. I didn't read it . . . not that I can. But perhaps it was wrong of me to bring it. Perhaps a prisoner shouldn't write to a lady.'

She lifted her eyes from the photograph and looked at me determinedly.

'No, Yanis, you did exactly the right thing. There is goodness in everyone if only we cared to see . . . Poor, poor man—if we cannot give hope to one in his situation, we can at least offer our friendship.' She slipped the photograph up her sleeve. 'If I write some words of comfort to him, will you deliver the letter? I will leave it in the trunk of the old hollow tree in the garden, you'll have no trouble finding it, there is only one such tree. And if . . . and if *he* should ever care to write again to me, leave any note or letter there also, so that I may claim it whenever circumstances allow—'

'*Countess.*'

Miss Mirsky's voice boomed along the hallway. We both jumped; the Countess turned to her, her shoulders drooping.

'Miss Mirsky, why, you quite startled me.'

'Perhaps if you weren't so taken up with whispering on the doorstep, you would have heard me approach.'

'*Whispering*, Miss Mirsky; you make me sound like a common criminal. Yanis is a dear sweet boy and I was merely—'

Miss Mirsky grunted and glanced down at her watch.

'Half past. Time for our afternoon tea.'

And gripping the Countess by her elbow, she marched her off like a powerful matron about to administer some disagreeable treatment.

Left alone in the hallway, I suddenly realized that it smelt different, that over the heavy fragrance of beeswax came the smell of cooking meat. It was the best smell in the world. And it reminded me that this evening Mrs Kropotkin was giving her dinner in honour of her *special* guests.

Dr Gomarus returned from the prison and flung his notebook on the side and cast himself into the chair opposite.

He pushed up his spectacles and rubbed his tired eyes, and made it quite clear he did not want to dine with anyone.

'There is so much to do, to write up; and you will miss another day at your letters and reading.'

'Oh, one day won't hurt.' I shrugged.

I filled a bowl with water and reluctantly he washed at it, ridding himself of the stale prison smell; then I helped him to dress.

'Hold still,' I said trying to knot his tie.

'What's the point, eh, Yanis? I am useless at these *civilized* occasions. Absolutely useless. And the talk all empty and silly and meaningless.'

'Colonel Zhuk will be there. You can talk about the prisoners and prison things.'

'It's hardly fit conversation for the dinner table, is it now? And that German Prince, he'll be there too, I suppose? And I'll tell you straight I don't care for the fellow one little bit. Not what I've seen of him so far, at any rate. You'd think he was at home in his castle the way he struts around, with that Tabrezian servant trailing behind like the family ghost. And he's *so* rude. He only speaks if he wants to know something.'

'There—'

I gave the tie a final smooth, pleased that Dr Gomarus disliked the German so much. This made us secret allies in the same campaign.

'Why are you smiling?'

'Oh—was I . . . ? Only because you look so smart.'

Mrs Kropotkin bustled everyone into their place; the German Prince at one end of the table, the Countess at the other.

Despite my trying hard not to, I kept looking her way. Stealing glances. For I don't believe I'd ever seen her look more beautiful than she did that night. Her hair and skin glowed, and her dark eyes gave away none of her secrets. She was dressed in yellow Japonaisie silk—buttercup yellow, my favourite colour; a simple embroidered spray of pink cherry blossom tumbling down from her shoulder.

So perfect that I felt proud just to know her.

In comparison the other diners seemed ordinary—and Miss Mirsky downright drab. But they all had a place at the table, even if it did seem they were arranged around the radiance of the Countess like beggars around a fire. I watched them from the corner of my eye. Miss Mirsky was situated next to the Prince, while Mrs Kropotkin herself came next and then Colonel Zhuk. Facing them were Mrs Zhuk and Dr Gomarus. I was permitted to sit by the fire and could see everyone's face, even those with their back to me, because of a large oval mirror on the opposite wall. Mrs Kropotkin promised if I sat there quietly I could have whatever was left over once the meal was finished.

She was the only one still not seated and fussed about the table a great deal, moving a candlestick a fraction this way or that, and straightening the cutlery. She had left Tonya manning the kitchen, and every few minutes or so you could count on the door flying open and Tonya blundering in, cow-eyed and tragic, to deliver her latest doom-laden message. 'Mrs Kropotkin—Mrs Kropotkin,

there's a funny smell coming from the oven.'
Or—'I've forgotten what you told me to do with
the potatoes, missus.'

And if Mrs Kropotkin was not dashing back to
the kitchen with Tonya, she was being summoned
upstairs by the *thud—thud—thud* of her husband's
walking stick on the floor above.

'Coming, my honey-sweet. Coming,' she would
cry, and go sweeping out of the room.

'Place is like a cheap beer garden,' growled the
German Prince, angrily flapping open his napkin
and draping it across his lap.

I watched all this from my perch amongst the
logs, seeing Dr Gomarus nervously smoothing
down the tablecloth in front of him, and Colonel
Zhuk glaring at his wife if she attempted any
small thing without his consent; she looking first
to her husband when Miss Mirsky asked her view
on the most trivial of matters; he displaying no
fondness in his look back.

Mrs Kropotkin returned from the latest
emergency, tilting her head awkwardly to give the
company her most reassuring smile.

'Mr Kropotkin dropped his hot-water bottle,'
she said sitting down with a breathless sigh. 'Got
himself into a real tizz—but I'm glad to say all is
well now.'

She rang a little silver bell to summon Tonya,

and the one time she was needed, Tonya did not come.

'Where is that girl?'

Up on her feet again, Mrs Kropotkin scuttled off towards the kitchen.

'God, I need a drink to get through this farce,' said the German Prince slumping back in his chair.

At this, Kazan, his serving-man, stepped from the shadows and moved silently around the table filling glasses with red wine. I observed him closely, this war hero from the Battle of the Goats. I saw that he was tall and stiff-backed, with an almost aristocratic bearing; his hair severely cropped. His eyes were every bit as dark as Tonya had said, and sharp and intelligent; and with the smallest of movements they managed to convey the subtlest of meanings.

He glanced questioningly towards the Countess, who covered her glass with her hand and shook her head, and Kazan moved on. Mrs Zhuk looked hopefully to her husband; he gave a curt shake of his head, but when his wife tried to cover her glass as the Countess had done, she clumsily knocked it over.

'See what you've done now,' hissed Colonel Zhuk venomously.

'Here. Fill me up, Kazan,' bellowed the German Prince waving his glass in the air.

The door opened and Mrs Kropotkin came in bearing a plate of pickled herring with dill and sour cream sauce; followed by Tonya with tiny triangles of bread and butter. They put the dishes on the sideboard for Kazan to serve, Tonya stepping back from him in undisguised horror.

'*Careful*, you silly girl, you'll knock over one of my best plates. If you want to be of some use, go put some more logs on the fire.'

Tonya did so, the logs more at home in her fat stubby fingers than some dainty piece of porcelain. As she viciously prodded the fire with the poker, she caught my eye, comically crossing her own eyes then rolling them upwards as if to say, 'Lord, what a performance.'

I smiled and she shot back a good-natured grin—and sang all the way down the hallway as she returned to the kitchen.

The meal began, the first course practically eaten in silence, despite Mrs Kropotkin doing her best to engage her guests in light conversation. But nothing ever came of it, each attempt fizzling out on her after a few inconsequential murmurings.

'Here, Kazan,' called the German Prince, 'keep watch, man, I'm practically dry.'

'That's right,' said Mrs Kropotkin uneasily. 'You must feel free to ask for whatever you like.'

With the first course finished, Mrs Kropotkin disappeared to the kitchen to supervise the next, and the Prince—so typical of his sort—left the table and came across and stood with his back to the fire, reading a newspaper. I drew in my legs, not out of respect for one of my betters, but because I couldn't stand him being so close to me.

His monocle gleamed as he thumbed through the pages, many of which were blocked out in printer's ink.

'Irksome this damn censorship business. You wait an age for news to come, and when the *Ursus* finally delivers it, everything of importance is blotted out. What's left, hmm . . . ? Society balls and advertisements for hair tonics.'

Colonel Zhuk fiddled with the button on his cuff.

'It is a necessary nuisance, I'm afraid, Prince, it stops useful information from falling into the hands of our enemies.'

The German Prince rattled his pages. 'You mean those revolutionary madmen? Heavens above, will somebody please tell me what is the point of them? *What is the point?* Troublesome pests, I call them. Like wasps and ants. I ask you, what was the good Lord thinking of when he conjured up wasps and ants? Hmm? They serve no useful purpose to anything but themselves; and those revolutionary fellows, are they *so* very different? Hmm? Hmm? You have a whole prison full of them, Colonel. They have free board and lodgings, with not a care in the world or a bill to pay.'

'It isn't quite like that—' began Dr Gomarus.

The German Prince drowned him out by rattling his pages even louder.

'They should all be strung up, I say. Every one of them. And good riddance.'

'Hear hear,' approved Colonel Zhuk, thumping the table hard with his fist.

'What about those in the forest?' asked Mrs Zhuk absently. She realized at once she had spoken out of turn and withdrew into herself in horror. Her husband glared.

'What's this?' asked Dr Gomarus. 'Revolutionaries in the forest?'

Colonel Zhuk reluctantly lifted his glare from his wife and laughed unconvincingly.

'Oh, it's nothing—nothing. Only some toothless old trapper—you know how those old-timers are—too much snow and drinking homemade vodka in their own company, crazy as bears. Claims he saw some armed men out in the forest the other day. Have no fear though. It's only vodka talk.'

'Course it is,' agreed the German Prince sounding oddly shaken. 'I mean, I'm out hunting in the

187

forest with Kazan most days. If anyone were to come across revolutionaries there, it would be us.'

'*Precisely*,' said Colonel Zhuk.

There the matter rested (for some not a second too soon—or so it seemed to me) for the door suddenly opened and Mrs Kropotkin reappeared, struggling to carry the next course—a great haunch of venison.

Her guests stared appreciatively.

'We were just talking about revolutionaries, Mrs Kropotkin,' said Miss Mirsky giving a nasty smile in the Countess's direction. 'Those unnatural creatures disloyal to our Tsar.'

Mrs Kropotkin handed the meat to Kazan and rejoined her guests, leaving him to carve, which he did expertly.

'Well, I don't really know much about politics,' she admitted. 'Nor do I care to. I just wish they would stop burning the churches. It's the poor priests I feel sorry for; it isn't nice. They are such unworldly men, I worry how they will survive.'

She twisted her head round as Tonya barged in, carrying a tray with dishes of carrots and potatoes and hot pickled red cabbage. She thrust it at Kazan and fled from the room, shrieking with terrified giggles.

Mrs Kropotkin threw up her hands.

'Oi, that girl.'

Miss Mirsky glanced across the table at the Countess, a predatory smile on her lips. And like a spider at the edge of its web, she lay in wait for her next opportunity to bait the younger woman again, seeing her chance come soon after when the Countess held up her hand and refused a plate of meat.

'*What*, you aren't eating, Countess? You really ought to, you know, when so many of our countrymen are starving and eat nothing but the bark off trees.'

I watched the Countess stare steadily at the table in front of her; her voice, when she spoke, quiet and commanding.

'Really, I'm not hungry, Miss Mirsky. Perhaps . . . perhaps in future I may be permitted to dine alone in my room?'

'*Nonsense*,' snorted Miss Mirsky. 'You need company. You need society—even if it is not the best society—' She remembered the German Prince and her eyes flickered wide with embarrassment. 'Forgive me, Prince. Naturally I did not mean you.'

'Hmm?'

The Prince was still in front of the fire reading his paper. Noticing that food had been laid out for him, he crossed over to the table and flung himself down, Kazan spreading a clean napkin across his lap.

The Prince picked up his knife and fork.

However, before commencing to eat, I saw how he stared at the Countess, her diamonds glittering in the candlelight and her head still bowed. If his intention was to cast her a smile, she was having none of it—and I was glad.

At midnight in my attic I pressed my hands together and prayed more fervently than I have ever prayed before.

'God bless the Countess,
Keep her strong and in health, and safe from those who do not wish her well.
The Mirsky is her first enemy:
May the Countess push her face into the snow with the toe of her slipper.
The Pig Prince is her second enemy:
May the Countess soon learn that bears have torn out his throat.
God bless me,
And help me serve her in every way I can.

Amen'

The following morning I found that the last part of my prayer had been answered—in the old tree, waiting to be delivered, a letter for Nikolay Kolchak . . .

From that time on, whenever we had a private moment together, the Countess called me her little postman. That was how I had come to see myself; not as the boy from the orphanage or Dr Gomarus's assistant—but as her little postman.

She wrote to Nikolay Kolchak almost every day—as he did to her; their letters becoming thicker and thicker. Nikolay Kolchak used the paper I had bought for him from the government store, and the Countess sent him some blank envelopes so that none of his pages went missing. When I asked the Countess in a roundabout way what he wrote, she laughed and said he often mentioned me. She said he called me 'that excellent fellow Yanis'.

What praise from so important a man.

One evening, after supper, Dr Gomarus and I were working alone in the library. It was very quiet with only an occasional rustle of paper or crackle of burning wood to disturb us. Dr Gomarus sat at the desk writing up his case notes, transferring them onto individual filing-cards, then filing them away in alphabetical order with my two photographs attached. He seemed dissatisfied. He kept sighing and crossing things out, at one point examining several of the callipers to see if they were bent or broken. I worked on the floor nearby, kneeling up to a chair, whose hard seat I used as a surface to rest upon as I practised my plurals.

My pen moved slowly across the paper.

The cat went up the tree
The cats went up the trees
The ship sailed into the rock
The ships sailed into the rocks

Dr Gomarus's desk was heaped and cluttered with reference books and the cabinet of glass eyes was open before him. Whenever the need arose, he pored over certain of its specimens, peering at them through a magnifying-glass and tilting the candle more closely to them so that little pimples of wax appeared on papers and books.

Between us, the doctor's magic lantern had been set up on a number of large atlases stacked upon a stool, a candle aglow inside. Above it, the heat rising from its metal casing made the air swirl all the way to the darkened ceiling, and floating dust caught in its beam of light was magnified a hundred times. Without a screen or patch of clear wall to project upon, the image from the lantern was thrown brokenly upon the spines of Mr Kropotkin's books—an image of twenty over-sized noses, their nostrils like arrow slits or niches in churches, the type meant for statues, or candles, or pictures of the Tsar.

Take the dog across the field
Take the dogs across the fields
The good shepherd shall watch the flock
The good shepherds—

'Yanis?'

I finished the line without hurrying.

—shall watch the flocks

'I have heard several surprising reports . . . that you have been spending rather a lot of time with that Nikolay Kolchak fellow.'

I looked up, startled to hear the doctor speak the name. First I wanted to lie—then I decided to be honest.

'Yes, I have. I've nothing else to do while I wait for you to finish taking the plates. And he's not a bit like I thought he'd be. He's kind and funny . . . You think it a bad thing?'

'Oh, no no. But . . . Yanis, you do realize that he is a condemned man?'

My nib dug into the paper and a large ink blob suddenly appeared. I was more furious than I had any real cause to be.

'I don't want you to get too fond of him, that's all,' said Dr Gomarus. 'It's only a matter of time and, well, you mustn't pin too much hope on him getting a pardon. I'm sure Nikolay Kolchak has faced up to the fact and is being realistic. You must too.'

'Do you forbid me to visit him?'

'No—heavens, of course not. You must do whatever you think fit, only, you must do it with your eyes wide open. Do you understand what I am telling you?'

The snake lay in the grass

'Well, Yanis?'

The snakes lay in the grasses

'Yes, doctor, I understand perfectly.'

I worked on but without enthusiasm or paying proper attention to what I did. I was thinking about the Countess and Nikolay Kolchak. Somehow they felt more real to me—more living, more human—

than Dr Gomarus and his dry scientific methods, surrounded by paper faces that were not even permitted a smile. In my mind I coldly and deliberately pushed him further away, made him more distant: even refusing to acknowledge all that I owed him.

I put down my pen, rose and spoke curtly.

'Dr Gomarus, if I might be excused for a moment.'

'You may, or you can use *my* chamber-pot if you so wish. You'll find it pushed under the bed.'

'No . . . I'd rather step outside if it's all the same to you.'

He shrugged without looking up, and I slipped away closing the door quietly behind me.

Outside, the raw cold bit through my coat. The snow, hardened with frost, gave reluctantly beneath my boots, making it difficult to walk. Pushing on, I made my way to the side of the house, the Countess's side, smiling when I saw that her unshuttered windows spilled out firelight across the garden, as rich and warm in colour as her Persian carpets. Inside, I spotted the Countess at once, and stepping back concealed myself behind one of the trimmed bushes flattened and misshapen by snow.

I watched her sitting on her elegant sofa, sewing, a deep red jewel gleaming at her throat.

Opposite her, Miss Mirsky was slumped back asleep, her knees apart and pulling at the fabric of her dress, her mouth an open gash and—although I heard nothing from within the room—I just knew that she was snoring.

My eyes hurried back to the Countess whose sewing strokes seemed to be getting slower and slower as if she were overtaken by her thoughts. Finally she stopped altogether, lifted her eyes from her needle and gazed across at her companion— and her look was one I hardly believed. It was so charged with an electrifying hatred that I gasped out '*Oh*', then swallowed the sound in surprise. In that, the briefest of moments, the Countess recomposed her features and with them again mild and unreadable, quietly went back to her sewing work as if nothing had taken place.

I scurried away, ploughing deeper into the garden, guiltily aware I had seen something I ought not to have done. I was glad that the darkness closed about me.

Soon I reached the cleared path. I went on until I came to the trees at the garden's furthest end. Above, I heard the branches creak with cold—it sounded like the trees complaining, the old gnarled ones muttering darkly. Wishing I had waited until morning, I peered ahead. As I did so, something caught my eye. I froze, my sense of disbelief giving way to the chilling realization I was not alone. Someone else was at the hollow tree.

Like me they had come without a lantern, braving the bitter cold. Like me they had no wish to be seen. But why . . . ?

My breath came raggedly and my brain emptied of every thought. Even so some instinct made me back away behind the nearest tree and press myself close to its trunk.

Seconds later a shadow flickered over the path at the very place where I had stood. It flickered and moved on—and only then did I find the courage to peer out after it. I saw a figure walking away. I knew who it was immediately. Those square shoulders, that straight back.

It was Kazan.

I watched him all the way to the house, and, sure that he was gone, I ran up to the hollow tree whose every part was familiar to me even in the darkness. The Countess's usual hiding place was empty, but lower down nearer the roots, my fingers closed around an envelope.

By its shape and feel I knew it was nothing to do with the Countess, and Kazan would have had no business writing to anyone. This left only one possible explanation. The letter that I gripped so tightly in my hand must be from the German Prince. Somehow he had found out about the tree. Now he was writing to the Countess. *Secretly.*

Roughly I scrunched the letter into my pocket, and with a savage glower on my face, returned to the house.

Steering clear of the library—not even bothering to poke my head around the door to bid the doctor goodnight—I went straight up to my attic where I lit the candle.

By its growing flame, I took out the crumpled envelope, handling it as I would something obnoxious.

I smelt it.

Tobacco.

I studied the writing on the front.

What was this? A jumble of pen-strokes that made no sense to me at all—but I decided that the style was a reflection of the writer's character—mean, spiky, and arrogant. Such a person deserved no consideration, still less his letter and whatever he had to say, and so without giving the matter further thought I tore the envelope open.

Spreading flat the single sheet I found inside, I was met by a solid block of writing similar to that on the envelope. Written in haste it seemed. And although I understood certain of the smaller words, the main part of the letter might have been in a foreign language for all the sense I could make of it.

Burning with frustration, I threw myself down on my mattress, only going back to the letter when I had calmed a little and was able to study it with a cooler eye.

This time I noticed that a solitary word stood out because it had been heavily underlined. For some reason it must be important. But what was that reason . . . ? With a stub of pencil I copied it out onto a scrap of paper as best I could, trying to tease out individual letters—but it was no use, I still couldn't read what it said. Growing frustrated again, I decided that a letter without meaning is a dead thing—and as a dead thing it deserved to be disposed of.

I felt a sense of power as I picked it up by a corner and held it over the candle. It took at once. I smiled at the flames as I watched them grow, and only when they threatened to burn me did I drop the letter on the floor and stamp it out.

The pleasing smell of burning lingered in the air as I changed into my nightshirt; the curled up ashes catching the draught of my movements as I slipped into bed.

A few days later and the unpleasantness in the garden was mostly forgotten. No further letters addressed in that spiky insistent writing turned up at the tree; and I saw less than the shadow of the Prince and his serving man, who were always off hunting before I rose.

This was no bad thing as far as I was concerned. What did concern me, however, was Dr Gomarus: he spoke no more about Nikolay Kolchak, yet the matter made us slightly awkward together. I know he didn't approve, but was resigned to the fact I would visit him (with or without his permission). Besides, I had a new reason to visit my prison friend now: he was teaching me to play chess.

Seeing me approach his cell that morning, Nikolay Kolchak lightly slipped off his bed, smiling his welcome, and placed the chessboard on the floor against the bars.

I knelt down to play.

'White or black?' he asked.

'White.'

'As always.'

We played a few moves before I became aware

of his eyes on me. I lifted my gaze and found it locked by his.

'You have anything for me today?'

I nodded.

'Top pocket.'

'Reach through the bars as if you're making a move.'

When I did so, he took the letter from me in one easy movement.

He looked down at it and smiled.

'What's this do you think? A letter from his majesty the Tsar? Dear Nikolay Kolchak, I pardon you for all your crimes against me, you shall not swing from a rope on my account.'

I know it is said that men facing death develop a grim sense of humour, it is just their way of dealing with it. Yet even so I found Nikolay Kolchak's light-hearted talk of his own death quite shocking. Instinctively I pulled away, but he caught my collar and roughly pulled me back, at the same time slipping his own letter into my now empty pocket.

He patted the place.

'For our friend the Countess,' he said smiling, but his blue eyes were hard.

His unexpected roughness upset me: it was almost as if the letter were more important to him than me. Then I heard him say, 'What's this?'

He picked up a scrap of paper. It must have come out with the Countess's letter. On it a single word—the one that I had copied down in my attic several nights before when it had seemed so important.

I made a lunge to snatch it back. He held it clear, smiling.

'Let me see. What does it say?'

He squinted up his eyes. '*In* . . . *In* . . . No—*implore*. A strong word, my friend, you must be careful how you use it.' He laughed and I angrily grabbed the paper off him, and he at last saw how it was with me.

'I'm sorry. I did not mean to tease you, Yanis.'

'It's nothing. Just a word. Nothing.'

'So why did you write it down?'

I shrugged indifferently.

'I saw it somewhere. I couldn't make it out, so I copied it. You know how it is. You know how much I want to learn to read and write.'

Nikolay Kolchak's mocking smile returned.

'So, tell me, was it in a love letter from that little maid you keep going on about? What's her name again?—Ah yes, Tonya. Did *she* write to you imploring you with all her heart? Well, Yanis, you're not denying it.'

I gritted my teeth.

'It wasn't from her and it wasn't in a love letter. *All right?* And I don't go on about her or anyone else.'

Nikolay Kolchak held up his hands in mock surrender.

'All right—all right. I'll say no more. Your move, I believe.'

We played on in silence, me badly, not really following the game but thinking other thoughts.

Nikolay Kolchak said, 'You know your trouble, Yanis? You always try to protect your queen; it weakens you all round.'

Later, with eight newly exposed plates in my carrying box, I trudged down the lane to the manor. My mood was grim, the words of Nikolay Kolchak going round in my brain. He had been joking, of course, and wrong about Tonya—but what if it had been the German Prince who was *imploring* the Countess with all his heart? What if the letter he sent to her, in secret, under cover of the night, was a love letter? If it had been, he had no business sending it. That cold-blooded snob didn't deserve the Countess for his wife. The man the Countess married ought to be far more handsome—someone warm, intelligent, and tender. Someone like . . . but that was impossible. Yet whoever it turned out to be it must *not* be the

German Prince, I would make certain of that; I owed it to the Countess for her kindness.

My thoughts ran on and on over the same territory and so preoccupied me that I hardly noticed anything else, certainly not the sound of raised voices or the church bell being rung as if by a madman. A moment later, however, I was overtaken by a group of altar-boys, running at full pelt, their deep-sleeved cassocks flying behind them as they raced down the lane.

'What's going on?' I called after them.

But they were too busy shouting to each other to notice me—and now they were gone. Sensing excitement in the offing, I wasted no time in sprinting after them.

Gaining a little, I saw them turn right, into the manor gateway, and seconds later had followed them through. There I came upon a puzzling sight.

The women of the house—the Countess, Mrs Kropotkin, Miss Mirsky, and Tonya—had gathered on the steps and were staring at the sight too. (Mrs Kropotkin, with her cheek pressed to a shoulder, resembled an indignant owl.)

The focus of everyone's attention were two horsemen halfway along the carriageway. I recognized the German Prince first, he was leaning heavily against his horse's flank. The other, watching him and still mounted, was Kazan; his eyes black and unemotional. The German Prince had just been violently sick in the snow and was groaning slightly as he rubbed his forehead against his horse's velvet coat.

I still didn't understand quite what I was seeing.

Behind the Prince's horse something had been tied, something that had been dragged back to the manor. It leaked blood into the snow, the pink stain spreading outwards and deepening to red.

At first I thought it a stag. But then, with a cold clutch of my stomach, I realized it was a man, his hands raised over his head as if (too late) in the act of surrendering.

I shook the shoulder of the nearest altar-boy.

'Who is it? Who's the man?'

The boy turned to me, his face lit with savage excitement.

'Some dirty revolutionary. The Prince came across him in the forest. The coward tried to ambush him, but the Prince shot him dead with a single bullet right through the heart.'

He grinned, and so help me I swear I could have knocked him down for his overbearing smugness. Standing still, I let the moment pass before turning back to the lifeless figure. I saw that he had been tied to the Prince's horse by his ankles and that one of his boots was half pulled off—cheap, poor men's boots that probably let in the cold and wet. It struck me as indecent. Someone should put it back on; someone should tie up the broken lace as once his mother would have done when he was small and young.

Around me the altar-boys whooped and yelped like a pack of hyenas. They dared each other and egged each other on until, for the sake of their own honour, they approached the Prince, raining down congratulatory pats on his back and making a general hubbub all about him.

With a violent jerk of his elbow he threw them off.

He bellowed at the top of his voice.

'*Kazan*—get me a drink, damn you!'

Kazan looked down at his master, speaking with his eyes. Asking him if his request was wise or sensible.

'*A drink*, Kazan.'

Unhurriedly Kazan dismounted and strode towards the house, the women on the steps standing aside to let him pass.

'I'll show you where I keep my medicinal spirits,' whispered Mrs Kropotkin, patting his wrist as if he were a helpless child.

When they reappeared, Kazan stepped forward into the garden alone, balancing a tray on his hand; on the tray a bottle and glass. The German Prince pounced upon him as soon as he was in range, grabbing the bottle and knocking the tray and glass into the snow. He tilted the bottle to his mouth and drank savagely, vodka trickling down his chin.

The altar-boys, meanwhile, not at all perturbed by the German Prince's furious outburst, had gathered around the dead man like those tiny scavenging creatures which swarm and feast upon a carcass of a bigger animal. They took solemn pleasure in prodding the body with sticks and nudging it with the toes of their boots. Then the black-robed priest appeared in the garden like a wounded crow, falling to his knees for dramatic effect.

'What is this?' roared the German Prince waving the bottle above his head. 'A Chinese circus? A comedy scene in a bad play?'

The priest crawled towards him on his knees, trying to catch his hand so he might kiss it.

'Sir, I tell you, you have done a great service today to those of us who love God and his Tsar— a great service.'

The German Prince glared at him, trembling with rage.

'You ape . . . Get off your knees. *Get up, I say!*'

He seized the priest by the scruff of his neck and hauled him to his feet—

'What does a poor excuse for a man like you know about anything? Hm?'

—and hurled him face first into the snow.

With that he stormed off towards the manor.

'Kazan, I'll be in my room. See you get rid of this rabble.'

Once he had gone, the women followed him inside, silently drifting away like mourners. Kazan remained behind and began clearing the garden, holding wide his arms and angrily flashing his eyes. Greatly in awe of him, the altar-boys moved off into the lane, clutching their prizes—buttons from the revolutionary's coat and bloodstained snowballs.

Hands on hips, Kazan stood in the gateway, watching them go; and feeling me watching *him*, turned smartly on his heels so that our eyes met over a distance: all his thoughts restrained by a steely will.

Then, as if I wasn't there, he crossed to the horses, loosened a strap or two and led them away to the stable. The dead man bumped along behind, his arms flailing in silent protest.

I shivered and gazed around. The garden was completely empty. I remembered the Countess standing pale-faced on the steps, and then I remembered Nikolay Kolchak's letter, and while the coast was clear, I set off to leave it at the hollow tree.

As soon as I was back in my attic I began work on Dr Gomarus's glass plates, keeping busy all the time, for it was only when I stopped that I thought about the dead man, wondering what Kazan had done with the body, if anything at all.

Later, when I went downstairs, I was surprised to catch Mrs Kropotkin and Tonya with their ears pressed to a door. From behind it I caught snatches of the German Prince's voice—his tone loud, slurred, and protesting.

I descended more slowly, trying not to make the stairs creak, gripping the handrail and hoping to slip by them unseen.

But Tonya caught my movement.

'The Prince is being interviewed by the secret police,' she whispered beckoning me across; and Mrs Kropotkin made room for me at the door, so it would have been far ruder not to join them there than to eavesdrop on what the Prince was saying.

Unsure, I put my ear up close to the cold wood, tuning in to the different voices.

First Inquisitor: So you shot him?

209

German Prince: Yes—yes, I told you so twenty times already.

Second Inquisitor: How many times, Prince, did you shoot him?

German Prince: Two—maybe three.

First Inquisitor: And you're quite sure you saw no one else there?

German Prince: Quite sure. The man was obviously a renegade working alone. All those rumours doing the rounds about a gang of revolutionaries camped out in the forest—it's sheer nonsense.

'Yanis?'

Hearing Dr Gomarus speak my name, I straightened guiltily, and Mrs Kropotkin and Tonya sprang away from the door, Tonya pretending to polish the handle with her elbow, huffing on it unconvincingly. I turned to face him. Home from the prison early, he had quietly let himself in with his key. He stood looking at me quizzically.

'Oh, doctor—doctor. You can't possibly guess what kind of day it's been,' cooed Mrs Kropotkin, twisting her handkerchief as if wringing it dry of tears.

She gathered us all up and swept us along to her small, back parlour, where Tonya flopped down in the most comfortable chair, curling her feet up under her like a cat, while Mrs Kropotkin served us hot sweet tea 'for our nerves'. Here

Dr Gomarus listened as we told him of the day's dreadful events.

'I've just had an awful thought,' said Mrs Kropotkin, breaking the reflective silence at the end. 'Do you think they will take our Prince away for what he has done? Do you think they will put him in prison?'

'I shouldn't think so, not for a moment,' said Dr Gomarus. 'What do you think, Yanis?'

'No,' I said, 'they're more likely to give him a big fat reward, a thousand draculs or more . . .'

Talking to the doctor so freely like this, well, it felt almost like it used to be, before Nikolay Kolchak put a cloud between us. We drank more tea and afterwards, as the doctor and I were climbing the stairs together, he suddenly turned to me and said, 'Yanis, I have something important to tell you.' Then he stopped, thin-lipped, and shook his head. 'No . . . let it wait until tomorrow.'

I awoke and sat up feeling sweat prickle along my hairline.

Gunshots . . . I heard—

Yes, there they were again. Loud. Crackling. Close to the house.

Then a shrill scream. *Tonya downstairs.*

I fumbled for my candle stub. Spilt the matches. Cursed. In the darkness—all thumbs and thudding heart. In fear another curse. The blankets caught up around my feet. Panicking now, I swept everything off the little cabinet and was forced to scrabble about the floor like a dog.

At last I found a match and managed to light it. Its flame stilled the moment, although my hand trembled as I lit the candle. The larger flame crackled and steadied. Half in fear I looked around expecting a rabble of leering revolutionaries.

Nothing. And the house again fallen ominously silent.

Desperate to find out what was going on, I got to my feet. My legs felt weak and unsteady as I crossed to the narrow attic stairs and descended, guiding my way with one hand on the wall, my stomach a ball of knots.

I emerged onto the landing. The library door was wide open and after a moment's panic I breathed out in relief, catching sight of Dr Gomarus standing in the doorway; his oil lamp on its shadowiest flame, a blanket around his shoulders.

'I heard—'

'I did too.'

We stood looking at each other. Dr Gomarus took off his spectacles and blinked his eyes. Then dumbly we both turned towards the main staircase. Someone was coming up. Weary feet and puffing breath. It did not sound like a sprightly revolutionary on his way to cut our throats, yet still we tensed, leaning towards each other and the comfort of the other's light.

Eventually, out of the darkness, the familiar hump-backed figure of Mrs Kropotkin appeared. She slumped heavily against the banister to catch her breath, and I noticed how Dr Gomarus pulled the blanket closer about him to hide his nightshirt.

Recovering, Mrs Kropotkin waddled towards us, shushing us as if we were responsible for the noise.

'Oh, my dears, my dears—'

'What is it, Mrs Kropotkin?'

'The German Prince. I fear he has been drinking more than is good for him.' She threw up her hands. 'Oi—oi.'

As she spoke, a burst of gunfire rang out, sounding twice as loud as it echoed up the panelled stairs. Mrs Kropotkin pressed a hand to her chest as if something was stuck in her throat, waiting for silence. When next she spoke, her voice had sunk to a whisper.

'Kazan is trying his best to calm him, but the Prince simply refuses to take any notice. He insists he will stay at his window until every dog is shot.'

'What dogs?' I asked.

'The village strays that creep into the garden every night to scavenge from our rubbish heap. Quite harmless in their beggarly way.'

A single shot interrupted her—after which we heard the Prince roar out, 'Let go of the barrel, Kazan, damn you—'

Mrs Kropotkin twisted her head round and gazed at us hopelessly.

'If this goes on much longer we shall have the secret police battering at the door—and isn't it bad enough that Miss Mirsky reports back everything that goes on already? Poor Tonya has locked herself in the pantry. She's refusing to come out. Ah well . . . Goodnight, doctor. Goodnight, Yanis. Such a trial—and my poor husband a bedridden invalid and his stomach a ruin.'

Sadly she turned and shuffled back down the stairs, knowing each step so well that she didn't need a candle to light her way.

Below us, the German Prince no longer raged, his mood turned to one of drunken self-pity.

'Damn this life, Kazan. Damn everything in it,' rose his voice like a sob.

Dr Gomarus caught my eye.

'May the good Lord protect us from our protectors,' he murmured softly, and turned and went back to his bed.

Somehow, I thought, with all that had gone on, Dr Gomarus and I had moved a little closer than we had been of late. But next morning as we walked towards our work at the prison, he seemed more distant than ever, and for the first time since leaving the orphanage, I felt uncomfortable in his company. Neither of us spoke; I kicked the snow resentfully, while he kept glancing ahead.

'Yanis, before we go any further, there is something you have to know.'

Dr Gomarus's tone was so grave that I looked at him in surprise. Then I remembered how he had wanted to speak to me on some important matter the day before but had decided to put it off.

'That prisoner. The one you've grown so attatched to. You know who I mean.'

'Nikolay Kolchak?' I would say his name if the doctor wouldn't. 'What about him?'

'Well, yesterday, shortly after you went back to the house, news arrived that his pardon has been turned down. There can be no further appeals. And, to be quite blunt, Yanis, they intend to hang the man before the end of the week.'

I felt a tightening at the back of my head; from it a cold trickling down my spine.

'Why didn't you tell me this before?'

'There was nothing you could do. Besides, with all that business with the German Prince, I judged it not the time. But now I have told you. Now you know.'

I stared ahead. My first thoughts were of the Countess. Who would tell *her*? I imagined the solemn words coming from my mouth and the tears welling up in her eyes. I thought about her so hard that I could smell her perfume.

The sound of hammering roused me and made me look up, surprised to find my vision swimming in tears. I sniffed and wiped them away.

I saw that we were just coming out of the high-banked lane into sight of the village.

There was more activity than usual.

The hammering stopped and started again. It drew my attention to a group of soldiers busily erecting a crude wooden structure beside the prison gateway.

I knew what it was as soon as I saw it, and the breeze turned icy upon my face.

It was a scaffold.

Now I understood why Dr Gomarus had kept glancing ahead as we walked up the lane, he was holding back the news till the last possible moment. Beside me I heard him mutter to himself.

'Such an unscientific way to end a man's life.'

Suddenly the anger that I had tried so hard to contain burst out of me. I could have flown at him with my nails for his heartless words. But instead of going to my hands, this wild ragged energy shot like fire down my legs, and I went scrambling away towards the prison as fast as I could go.

Prison security that morning was as lax as ever. Nobody demanded to see my pass and I wouldn't have stopped if they had. On the stairs, a couple of guards mockingly pressed themselves close to either wall as I thundered up between them, one calling out after me, 'What's the rush, son? The prison riot isn't due to start for another hour.'

On reaching Nikolay Kolchak's corridor, the father and son warders greeted me almost in tears.

'Such a crying shame,' said the elder one. 'Nikolay Kolchak is one of nature's gentlemen. We need to bring more men like him into the world, not send them out. If only he could have got his politics straight and been one of us.'

'That's the trouble with this country,' said the younger one bitterly. 'We waste all our time and effort fighting each other when we have enemies enough at the borders. It's a tragedy.'

He took out his handkerchief and dabbed his eyes.

'Can I go and see him now?' I asked.

'Yes—yes. Go. You'll be fine company. Try to keep his mind off the rope.'

Tears began to prick their eyes once more, so I hastened on.

The way to Nikolay Kolchak's cell was well known to me, but today I was aware of each and every step I took along it. I approached in reverent awe as if to a holy man, and when I got there I saw that the black skull had been painted over in red, wet paint dribbling blood-like down the bars.

'Yanis—why, how splendid.'

Nikolay Kolchak met me at his cell door, his greeting never more cheerful.

'What do you think, eh? As soon as I have a date with the hangman, they double my rations and give me a tot of vodka to help me sleep at night.' He laughed and shook his head disbelievingly. 'What a crazy old world this must be when those condemned to death are treated better than those condemned to life and living.'

Without explanation or bothering to conceal it, I thrust the Countess's latest letter through the bars at him. He slowly glanced down at it, smiled, and gave me a quaint little bow before taking it and putting it under his pillow. From the same place he took the letter I must take away with me.

I gripped it in my hand.

'Oh, Nikolay Kolchak—I shall pray for you every day. Really I shall.'

He threw back his head and laughed.

'You do that, Yanis. Pray for a miracle, because it's quite useless praying for a pardon any more.'

I had to leave Nikolay Kolchak soon after (the governor was paying a call), so reluctantly I came away and went to find Dr Gomarus, at work in a different part of the block. The doctor showed no surprise at seeing me there, but neither was he inquisitive enough to question me. Perhaps all the answers he needed were written on my face.

My mood was restless. I kept sighing and shuffling my feet and gazing longingly towards the barred outer windows. The morning to me seemed endless.

The doctor, as he measured the circumferences of heads and recorded the shapes of ears, was at first distracted by my fidgeting, then so irritated that at last he shoved the familiar little mahogany box into my hands and said, 'Here, Yanis, four plates instead of the usual eight. Go and start work on them. It may give your mind something else to focus on.'

I took them gratefully.

'Yes, doctor. Of course, doctor. At once.'

And with that I was gone.

Outside, I stopped a moment near the scaffold. It was nearly completed. The soldiers who were building it laughed and joked amongst themselves, and the priest hovered nearby like the carrion crow who follows the wolves.

Seeing him smirk at some grim joke, I came away sickened to my stomach, and I did not look back until I reached the manor grounds.

I walked quickly and purposefully, yet as I drew level with the second tree, a hand roughly grabbed me from behind and I dropped the box of plates. Taken unawares, I was pulled from the track, thrown on my back in the snow and pinned there—my ambusher sitting astride my chest.

Shock turned to fury when I saw it was Tonya.

'*Get off me*,' I snarled through gritted teeth. I struggled but she was a powerfully built girl who kept me down with ease. She flicked my nose.

'Told you I could wrestle you and win.'

'That's not fair—you took me by surprise.'

I ranted on at her, but Tonya wasn't listening, she was gazing around like an animal that catches an unexpected scent.

She bent forward and spoke in a whisper, her breath smelling of stale coffee.

'Shall I tell you a secret?'

'Can't stop you, can I, when you're sitting on my chest.'

She slapped my shoulder.

'No, *listen*, it's important . . . He's here.'

'Who is?'

'The hangman, of course, stupid. He's in the house right now.'

'Why?'

'Because nobody else'd put him up, so Colonel Zhuk asked Mrs Kropotkin as a special favour, knowing full well she's daft enough not to say no to him. Anyway, the hangman must have been waiting outside because a few minutes later he arrived with his bag.'

'And he's staying as one of her guests . . . ? *Where?* There isn't room.'

My voice rose in panic. For one terrible moment I thought the hangman might be forced into sharing my attic.

'Oh yes, there is. The cubby-hole next to the boiler. It's no bigger than a broom cupboard, but he's happy to have it. The missus said, "Tonya, help me get a camp bed in", but I said I wouldn't lift a finger to help no hangman. He's having all his meals there too. He's told Mrs Kropotkin that no one will ever know he was there, he'll be like a mouse. No one will ever see him come or go. But then I've told Mrs Kropotkin that the same might be said of the Angel of Death.' She rubbed her arms as if cold. 'Gives me the creeps it does. And I've told the missus I won't stay a minute more under the same roof as him.'

'So what will you do?'

She shrugged.

'Go somewhere else, I suppose. I'll go to my sister's in the village; that is, if she'll have me. She rows with her husband all the time and he gets drunk and smashes things, and with six kids, I'll have to sleep in the ashes of the fire. But better that than stop here.'

I saw that her eyes were filling with tears and struggled in disgust as they fell on me freely and heavily.

'Take care, Yanis, my sweetheart.'

Then to my astonishment she suddenly bent down and kissed me wetly on my forehead, before springing up and fleeing the garden as if pursued by the hangman shaking his noose.

Slowly I picked myself up and brushed myself down, deciding not to worry about what Tonya had just told me: time enough for that later. Besides, I had a more pressing matter on my mind.

I went and found Dr Gomarus's little carrying box, and with it gripped firmly in my hand, continued up the carriageway to the front door. I hammered loudly on it, and when Mrs Kropotkin opened it, I said in a voice that even to my ears sounded unnaturally bright and piping, 'Why, good afternoon, Mrs Kropotkin. It's me. I'm back from the prison good and early today.'

Mrs Kropotkin screwed her head round and gave me a curious look.

'So I see, dear.'

But how was she to know that my real reason for grandly announcing myself was to alert the Countess to my being there. Then I became aware that Mrs Kropotkin was moving in a series of strange little jerks and realized she was trying to stand on tiptoe to see over my shoulder into the garden. It seemed neither of us was the one who the other really wanted it to be.

'She's gone to her sister's,' I explained.

Exhausted by the effort of trying to see past me, Mrs Kropotkin let her gaze fall back to the floor.

'Silly, silly girl. And I've baked her an apple cake as a special treat. Her favourite. *Oi*—but enough of that, come in, my dear.'

I stepped inside and Mrs Kropotkin closed the door.

'Of course, she will have told you the news. The girl is such a terrible gossip, can't keep a single thing to herself.'

I loosened my scarf and nodded.

'She did have a few things to say. Let me see, there was something about a new gentleman . . . Mrs Kropotkin, what is he like?'

Forgetting what she had accused Tonya of a moment before, Mrs Kropotkin stopped to consider.

'Small, I would say. Ordinary. Very good teeth. He would pass for an honest tradesman if you knew no better.' She stared sadly at the door. 'But Tonya's trouble has always been she is too superstitious for her own good. I tell you, she has only to see a black cat and she refuses to go outside to fetch the logs in.'

Waddling like a duck, Mrs Kropotkin side-stepped round to get me back into her sight. 'But you're not a superstitious boy, are you? Now, what would you say to a nice cup of tea and a big slab of apple cake fresh from the oven?'

I could tell she was desperate for a bit of company, but just when I was on the point of declining, there came an insistent *thud—thud—thud* on the ceiling above.

'Oh, there goes Mr Kropotkin again. I shall have to see what he wants. Probably his spectacles. He loses them in the bedclothes, you know. I'll just . . .'

I watched her bustle away up the stairs, happy to be occupied, and when I could no longer hear her voice or footsteps, I slipped through the house and out of the back door. In the garden I 'posted' Nikolay Kolchak's letter and afterwards, instead of turning away, I crept around the back of the hollow tree and there, out of sight, I waited.

Almost at once it began to snow, at first in gritty grains no bigger than sugar, but soon blossoming into strange feathery flakes that were so light and dry that they crumbled to nothing upon impact.

They covered me in their remains as if with dust, and it grew colder. My feet and hands . . . Why didn't she come? *Why?* Was Miss Mirsky proving difficult? Was she stubbornly putting off her afternoon nap? And then there were the plates that Dr Gomarus was expecting to find finished into photographs. Five more minutes, I would give her five more minutes, that was all I could allow.

And then through the curtain of silently falling snow she appeared. Her heavy fur coat swayed around her ankles, and she bowed her head to keep the flakes from her eyes, her fur hat turning white, even as I watched.

That was all I did. *Watch*. She came up close until only the hollow tree separated us. I pressed my back to its trunk, hearing her joyful murmur as she discovered the waiting letter. Moments later she wandered back into view and I guessed she was returning to the house; my mouth fell open ready to call her, but she stopped at the next tree. Taking shelter there, she tore open the envelope and, standing perfectly still, began to read.

I saw her shoulders slump and knew she had learnt from Nikolay Kolchak himself of his fate; her arms slowly going down to her sides, the crumpled letter in one hand.

I could bear it no longer.

'Countess . . .'

I stepped into view.

Immediately she was back on guard; she spun round to face me, peering hard through the falling snow.

'Yanis? Is that you?'

I brushed off what I could to show her that it was.

'You know now, don't you?' I said.

She nodded slowly. 'When will it . . . ?'

'The day after tomorrow.'

'*So soon?*'

'I'm very sorry, Countess.'

Her eyes gleamed almost yellow as she strode across and held the tops of my arms in her hands. It felt nice being so close to her; not like it was with Tonya. But why go and think of *her* at this time? Why remember Tonya when it was the Countess who mattered?

She began to speak, her words pouring out as if to keep her emotions under control.

'You will go to the prison again tomorrow, Yanis? Of course you will. You go every day. Nikolay Kolchak must look forward to your daily visits. How I wish that I could visit him there too. But no, that isn't possible. I have come to know him instead through his charming courteous letters. I believe I know him as well as you, Yanis.

And just thinking about him . . . see, it brings me to the verge of tears. No, no, I am quite all right, thank you. But I feel I can't just abandon the poor man now. It's inhuman. Yanis, there is something I want you to take to him. Something to make his last few days on earth more bearable. It is my favourite icon—the one of St Jude. Will you take it to him in prison, to comfort his final hours? Will you? It would mean so much. Tell him he will find peace of mind in it. Tell him that. I will leave it by the hatstand in the hallway. It will be there waiting for you in the morning. You *will* take it to him, won't you? You will, promise me you will . . . ?'

'Countess, I . . .'

'Of course you will. I know you will. You are a dear, dear boy . . . I have to go now. Miss Mirsky and . . . well . . . Remember the icon, Yanis. *Remember.*'

And I saw tears trickling down her cheeks as she turned and hurried away.

Standing there in the garden, without a breath of wind or a friendly light visible from the house, I felt lost and all alone in the world—just the snow falling down and the Countess's footprints vanishing from sight, flake, by flake, by flake.

That night I lit a candle and prayed.

'God bless Nikolay Kolchak,

K-keep him—'

I got no further, but curled up into a tight ball like a baby.

The hatstand in the hall was a grotesque piece of work—a rearing bear attacked by bats. The bear was larger than life-size and carved from an almost black wood; the brass bats served as hat pegs. It was the kind of thing that, once seen a few times, you instinctively avoided, either out of fright or good taste, so anything tucked away at its side would never be noticed unless you went out of your way to look for it. Coming downstairs to breakfast the following morning, my gaze fixed unblinkingly on it, and sure enough I saw something there: a flat case with a rope handle, the icon (I supposed) folded away inside.

I wondered when the Countess had managed to put it there. Had Miss Mirsky taken another nap after supper? Or had the Countess crept out of bed under cover of night, feeling her way around half-remembered obstacles?

I left it where it was until after breakfast, when it was time to set off for work. Then, matter of factly, I picked it up (it was heavier than I expected), wary of being asked by Dr Gomarus what it was and having to explain. Of course he noticed it immediately but waited until we were well on our way before making any mention of it.

'What's that you're carrying, Yanis?'

He was looking at me through his pink spectacles rather than at the case.

'An icon, sir.'

'An icon—*really*? But why?'

'For the last hours of Nikolay Kolchak. For him to pray to.'

'Did Mrs Kropotkin give it to you?'

'No, sir.'

I was deliberately and stubbornly unforthcoming.

'Who then?'

'The Countess.'

'The Countess? But why should she care anything for Nikolay Kolchak?'

'Because she is a good woman. Because I told her about Nikolay Kolchak and his story moved her. Because that is the way good people are.'

I had not meant my tone to be critical of him for doing nothing—but somehow it was there, and I knew he was wounded by it and would not probe any deeper, and I felt a little ashamed of myself. To put my mind off the matter, I thought of Nikolay Kolchak alone in his cell, anxiously wondering when I would come.

At the prison the doctor and I went our separate ways, me to discover that the father and son team were not on duty that day. In their place was a fat man with a small square moustache like a patch of velvet between his top lip and nostrils. He sat eating a hock of pork, his handkerchief tucked into his collar.

'What have you got there?' he asked gruffly.

'Nothing—an icon for the condemned man. A lady has sent it to comfort him.'

With a grunt the warden lowered his eyes to his food, losing what little interest he had in me, and so I was able to continue on to Nikolay Kolchak's cell.

He took in my arrival with a blank stare, his face grey and unsmiling as if he did not recognize me, nor did he rise from the bed where he lay, devoid of any energy. Unwashed and unshaven, he looked thinner and older all in the space of a few hours, and I felt a frightening coldness go through me.

'Is the scaffold ready yet?'

I nodded. 'They were busy brushing snow off it just now so that no one would slip and hurt themselves.'

I thought the grim humour of my news might appeal to him, but he hardly noticed and I wished I had not been so flippant. I seized on the icon.

'*Look.* I have something for you. From the Countess. It's an icon of her favourite saint. She begged me to bring it to you and she says I am to tell you to find peace of mind in it.'

He slunk off his bed like a sick man, a blanket around his shoulders, and lurched over to me; and taking the case through the bars without a word, he threw himself back down upon his bed.

He began to mumble something, his lips sticky with white mucus. It took me a while to realize fully what he was saying.

'Go now, Yanis. Go back to Dr Gomarus. Go from here and forget about me. Forget you have ever known me or looked upon my face.'

'*Forget you . . . ?*'

He clutched the icon to his chest, his eyes closed. I waited for him to speak again and when he didn't I backed slowly away, convinced he would change his mind and call me back and beg me to stay.

I counted my steps.

I lingered a moment at the door, the warder suspiciously watching.

But Nikolay Kolchak never so much as whispered my name, and so I turned away and left that place for the very last time.

I awoke with a great gulp of air as if drowning: the darkness of my attic like a deep body of water piled up over me. Then I remembered where I was and that I had been dreaming of Nikolay Kolchak—and that this was the morning they were going to hang him . . .

I dressed and went down the attic stairs, stepping out into the cold early morning light of the landing. The light came from a tall window which also gave a clear view over the front garden; more snow had fallen in the night, and up the carriageway I saw a fresh set of footprints leading away. These couldn't belong to Dr Gomarus—nor Mrs Kropotkin, who I could hear talking to her husband in that special part-cross, part-baby-coo way she always spoke to him. Tonya had left and gone to her sister's, and if the Countess or the German Prince had gone any further than the grounds, she or he would surely be accompanied by Miss Mirsky or Kazan respectively; besides, the German Prince had not strayed past his door for days now.

So if the tracks of this early bird didn't belong to any of these, they could only belong to the one person who remained—the hangman, off to perform his ghoulish duty at the prison.

I shuddered.

'What? Cold, Yanis?'

I half turned and saw Dr Gomarus.

'No, not really.'

'I didn't expect you up so soon. Don't you remember? I told you yesterday, the prison is closed to visitors today on account of . . . on account of what is taking place there. You may as well have the day off, I shan't be needing you. I intend to bury myself away in the library till supper, reading. You can stay here and practise your writing, if you like—or go up to the village . . . that is, if you really wish to do so.'

He picked his words carefully, and in the air hovered many unspoken meanings.

'Perhaps,' I mumbled. 'Thank you, doctor.'

I wasn't hungry and felt unable to face Mrs Kropotkin's unrelenting cheerfulness over the breakfast table for the sake of a cup of coffee, so quietly I pulled on my boots and coat and stepped outside, the frosty air tasting bitingly pure after the staleness of the house.

Without meaning to, I started to follow the hangman's footprints, astonished by how small they were. In size they were more like a child's than a fully grown man's, and by turns I imagined him as a malignant bloated baby or as a goblin, his face covered in puckered skin, skipping up the lane and gloating over his power to bring misery.

By now my feverish thoughts had brought me to the outskirts of the village where the footprints became lost amongst the dirty trampled snow. About me I sensed an air of restrained excitement, more fitting for a carnival than a public execution. Booths had been erected and already some idle men were drinking more than they ought. I forced myself to go closer to the scaffold, joining the crowd who watched the last-minute preparations to ensure that everything went smoothly; after all, a scaffold is only a stage and a hanging another kind of show. To that end, a practice run was being held, with a sack of turnips taking the condemned man's place, while the main business talk concerned *sway* and *slack* and the sinister sounding *dead weight*. Nothing was left to chance. With the kind of care I had seen only Dr Gomarus take, everything was checked and properly positioned, until the moment was ready. Then with a heart-stopping bang the trapdoor fell open and the rope creaked as it strained under the sack's weight. A cheer went up and those who did not cheer laughed nervously.

Hardly had the sack ceased swaying when four men hoisted it back up for a second try, while two others knelt to oil the hinges of the trapdoor. I studied each man carefully, trying to work out which, if any, was the hangman. I had imagined I would recognize him at once by a certain air that set him apart. But these men seemed like ordinary workmen; and what difference did it make if I recognized him or not? It would not stop Nikolay Kolchak from being hanged. Despondently I turned away, and pushing through the crowd made my way out of the village.

'You there—*boy*!'

I lifted my eyes to see Miss Mirsky lurching towards me, her figure as lumpy and ungainly as ever. She appeared in a high state of excitement, carrying a small picnic hamper in one hand and a collapsible chair in the other.

'Where are you going?' she demanded breathlessly, little flecks of spit striking my face.

'Back to the manor; my master has work I have to finish.'

The lie came easily, and I was able to meet her eye without a blink of discomposure.

'How tiresome. You should turn on your heels and go straight back to the village this instant. You should witness for yourself how the Tsar's justice is served. A young boy like you; why, it would do you the world of good, and I'm sure your master wouldn't grudge a few minutes so well spent.'

'*No*—I have to go. Really I do.'

I began to edge away, glad that her hands were full, otherwise I felt sure she would have dragged me along with her.

She glanced down at her bosom, which made an ideal ledge for her watch, and tutted.

'How time gets on. Ah, I suppose I must make tracks if I am to be sure of a good position. Long live the Tsar!' And saying this she wheeled around and lumbered off up the lane like someone dashing to catch a train.

The air seemed more wholesome once she had gone.

I returned to the manor, but instead of knocking at the main door went all the way round the house to the kitchen whose door was never locked. I let myself in. Judging by the bowls and spoons and floury surfaces, Mrs Kropotkin was halfway through baking but had been called away—probably by her husband—giving me an opportunity of going straight to the Countess's room without being seen.

Hardly had my knuckles brushed her door, when it flew open and she stood before me. Seeing who it was, she opened the door wider and let me in.

Her drawing room was in darkness, the curtains pulled to, the only light coming from a huge log fire whose heat immediately made my face glisten with sweat. Flames roared up the chimney and the violent orange light pursued shadows around the walls.

Urgently she turned to me.

'What time is it?'

The black elephant clock was just as close to her as it was to me, but she appeared to have forgotten it.

'Twenty to ten, Countess. There's just twenty minutes to go.'

She began to pace the room, wringing her hands.

'I tell you everything is rushing around in my head—nothing is still. And do you notice how cold it is? I simply cannot get warm. My blood is like water. Throw some more logs on the fire, Yanis. Call Mrs Kropotkin and have her get some more.'

I approached the fire, cowering before its fierce furnace-like heat. Despite a plentiful basket of wood nearby and the Countess's request, there was no need or room to add more fuel, so I knelt to prod the burning logs. The clock struck quarter to and the Countess stopped a moment to gaze at it quizzically.

Her face was beautiful in the firelight.

Then too late I realized the poker was burning my hand and threw it down with an unnecessarily loud clatter. Mortified, I lifted my head to apologize, but saw that the Countess hadn't so much as glanced my way. Pushing the poker aside with my boot, I retreated to a chair where I could watch her prowl. The clock ticked on and every now and then either she or I glanced towards it, sometimes one of us setting off the other as with a yawn. Even so, the Countess never quite seemed able to believe her own eyes.

'What time is it, Yanis?'

'Ten minutes to, Countess.'

She paced on, scratching at her arms and neck. And I thought how strange it was that she, who refused to stand up for a tsar, now found it impossible to sit down for a condemned rebel.

'And now what time is it?'

I wiped my sweating brow on the back of my hand.

'Only a minute after you last asked, Countess.'

'Is it—is it really? You could have said a whole hour had gone by and I would have believed you. Or you might have told me that time had ground to a halt and I shall be forced to go on walking up and down in this wretched room for an eternity, like one of the restless dead who can find no peace . . . I'm sure today must be the coldest day, I'm sure there must be a great blizzard coming. Are the curtains drawn properly, Yanis? Is a draught creeping in?'

Although I thought it unlikely, I crossed to the windows and made a show of checking, fussing with the curtains; all the time her moving shadow flickering on the walls and ceiling.

'What time is it now, Yanis?'

'Five minutes to ten, Countess. It is very close.'

The resin in the logs fizzled and spat, and the Countess clawed at her neck like an animal at a wound. I could see red nail-marks on her fair skin and grew more concerned for her.

'Countess, do you not think you should sit down before you wear yourself out? I could fetch some tea.'

'*Tea.*'

She stopped and looked at me then burst out into a harsh brittle laugh.

'Tea? What use is that to anyone? Honestly, at times you sound like Mrs Kropotkin, Yanis. Tea will make everything better, will it? The great cure-all.'

She laughed again, verging on hysterical—then stopped abruptly. For the clock's chiming mechanism had begun to whirl, catching us both unawares, and now in silence we counted each stroke.

. . . *seven . . . eight . . . nine . . .*

Then distantly from the village arose a mighty roar.

240

For an hour afterwards we sat in silence, the darkness gathering around us as the flames died back. Then we heard Miss Mirsky return, boorishly singing patriotic songs as she trudged up the carriageway, and it awoke us from our sad dreams.

The Countess stirred first.

Without a word, she crossed to the mirror to examine her face. She was much calmer now. I could tell she did not want Miss Mirsky to see her in her present state; she ran her fingers beneath her eyes and pinched her cheeks to make them rosy. And taking a silver brush from a nearby bureau, she began to work upon her hair.

Surprised and embarrassed that she did so before me, I jumped up feeling I was intruding.

'Shall I leave you, Countess?'

She went on brushing her hair, a lock at a time, her eyes watching me closely in the mirror.

'Yani, dearest boy, will you do one last thing for me—for Nikolay Kolchak?'

'Name it,' I said, but sounded puzzled. What more could be done?

She continued speaking, in a slow measured way that matched each brush stroke.

'I've heard that his body is to be taken to a small out-building behind the church. The high-minded priest won't allow it into his neat, whitewashed building, so there is nobody who will pray for him or think of him kindly, even though he is dead. Imagine that, Yani, nobody who cares—the thought makes me tremble. But you and I, Yani, we can change all that. We can do one last little thing for him to show that someone *does* care. I want you to go to that place behind the church and lay two coins over his eyes, which is a custom permitted even the meanest of beggars. Will you do that for him, Yani? Will you do that for Nikolay Kolchak?'

Coins . . . ? Eyes . . . ?

I was slow to understand.

She turned to face me, her hand outstretched. For a moment I thought she wanted me to kiss it. Confused, I put out my own hand, and as it came up to hers, she dropped something into my palm.

Two copper coins.

'You will do this for me, Yani, won't you? You won't let me down? But not now. Not with so many people around. Go as soon as it gets dark. Go under cover of nightfall.'

Her voice was both soft and persuasive.

For the rest of the day I was unable to do anything but think of what lay ahead once nightfall came. The air in the house seemed hot and stale, giving me a dull headache as if from sleeping too long, yet every few minutes I yawned. Finally, though, it was time. Creeping downstairs, I put on my boots and outdoor things and with a glance behind, slipped from the house.

The drop in temperature left me breathless and redoubled my headache with a sudden sharp pain. I steadied myself before going on, the steps cracking with frost; the snow in the darkness velvety grey.

I couldn't believe what I was doing.

I was setting off for the village with two copper coins in my pocket, meant for the dead eyes of a hanged man. Already the coins felt as if they belonged to another, unearthly world, and I could not bear to touch them or hear them jangle—just hearing the sound sucked the air from my lungs, and I felt their weight dragging on me like chains.

I was sweating by the time I reached the lane; in my head Dr Gomarus's voice kept telling me, 'Go if you must . . . ' Was this because I had lied to him, making up a lame excuse to explain why I needed to go into the village and miss supper? He had looked at me over his pink lenses and I could tell he didn't believe a word of it—and that was when he had said it. 'Go if you must,' and I had imagined all sorts of tones in his voice—of disapproval, sadness, disappointment. I felt ashamed that I was forced to lie to him, not least because he always set such great store by the truth. Truth and science, he said, are different sides of the same coin.

There, coins again. No escaping them tonight . . .

I paused to wipe my nose on the back of my glove; before me the familiar sight of the village, the garrison barracks on one side, prison walls on the other. Familiar—but tonight different too. For by the deserted scaffold a large bonfire had been lit, so large that its light reflected off the onion-shaped dome upon the church tower. People were dancing hand-in-hand around the flames, three rings of noisy jostling folk singing at the tops of their voices and almost drowning out the music of two accordion players, whose fingers flew across the stops.

Everyone appeared worse for drink. The women shrieked with laughter, and children, taking advantage of the soldiers' drunken sentimentality, held out their hands for coins.

If only it were possible I'd have gladly given them mine—like passing on a curse.

Of course, in my place, I knew what some would do. They would say they had carried out the Countess's wishes to the letter, when in fact they had kept the coins, or thrown them away, or given them to the poor if their consciences really pricked. The Countess would never be any the wiser; but be that as it may, I could never bring myself to do any of those things. Not to her. I could lie easily to Miss Mirsky, unwillingly to Dr Gomarus, but never in any shape or form to the Countess.

So I moved on, and keeping to the shadows turned down the alley at the side of the church where an overpowering smell made me wince. Under cover of darkness, men were using it as a urinal. Too drunk to stand, they leant one-handed against the church wall, grunting as acrid steam rose up into their faces.

I quickened my footsteps until I was safely past, then I stopped to listen. The rowdy noise had been left behind, and once more I became aware of the breeze as it stirred the scratchy snow.

My heart beat faster.

The only thing before me now was a small plain building set so far back from the rest of the village that it was practically in the forest.

Bound to my promise to the Countess, I pressed on, the trampled snow frozen hard and like badly laid cobbles beneath my boots.

As I drew closer to the building, I saw a movement in the shadows and immediately was on my guard. I watched, waiting for something to happen, jolting in surprise when it did. First a pair of emerald eyes flashed at me—then, swiftly following that, there arose a shrill banshee-like wail.

In panic I fought back the urge to flee . . . It was only a cat, I told myself. Listen, there it was again—see?—a cat calling its cousins.

The other cats came quickly once summoned—tails raised, running light-footedly—taking up their positions in the open. I sensed each cat keenly watching me with its bright eyes; the mournful cry taken up and passed on in turn between them.

Remembering that the last time I had seen so many cats together had been at the green clapper-board house, I guessed at their presence here now and gave an angry shout.

'Old woman! Hey, old woman, I know you're there. Step out where I can see you!'

'No call to make such a palaver, dearie.'

The filthy creature appeared unhurriedly from behind the building, pulling her shawls to, and straining her eyes to see who had called.

'You've no business to be poking around here. I know what you're up to. I know your game.'

'Do you, dearie, do you really? Is that the reason that brings you here too?' She answered quite calmly and made no attempt to conceal the incriminating crowbar in her hand. 'Maybe we can reach a little . . . deal between us.'

'I'll make no deal with you, you old leech. You think I've come to rob the dead? You think I would go through a dead man's pockets? Say that again and I'll call the soldiers to you. They'll know what to do with a dirty thief and her stinking cats. Now clear off before I change my mind and fetch them.'

Unprotesting, the old woman edged away, turning on me a sickly fawning smile, her eyes red and rheumy with the cold.

'No need for unpleasantness, my dear. No real harm done. None at all. See, we are on our way, aren't we, my sweets?'

The cats poured after her yowling as with one voice.

I watched her go, shouting and throwing lumps of ice at her each time she glanced back, wanting more than anything for her to provoke me. After all, better to be angry than afraid. But she hurried away and when she had gone my sense of unease was just the same.

Stop being a baby, I told myself. Stop being a coward. Only a kitten jumps at its own shadow. If an old woman can do it, why not you? And it's not as if I hadn't seen death before. At the orphanage some fever or other was always carrying off one of Mrs Pafnutkin's mites. Washed and tidied, in an open casket, it was the only time an orphan ever looked vaguely healthy.

Carried forward on a surge of bravery, I reached as far as the door. As suspected, the padlock lay broken in the snow. I gripped the door handle. To my surprise it turned with ease and the door rolled smoothly open.

Beyond lay a darkened room.

As I stood staring into it, stirred memories of the orphanage came flooding back. Now it was of the *Illiterates' Bible*, a book of brightly coloured pictures shown to us every Sunday evening. I remembered in particular 'the gateway to hell', the sinners drawn to a similar black portal—murderers and thieves, money-lenders, drunks, and those who did not pay their taxes . . . and revolutionaries, of course, the likes of Nikolay Kolchak.

And just as those sinners were unprepared for the moment, so too was I. I gave a cry of dismay.

'A candle—I should have brought a candle!'

It was too late to go back and the prospect of feeling my way blindly in the dark made my flesh crawl, but there was no other way.

Pulling off my gloves and steadying my courage, I took a step forward; then another, smaller step; then a smaller step still. A dreary greyish light followed me through the doorway, but by then my eyes were used to the dark.

Before me I saw a trestle table—on it the unmistakable body of a man, covered in sacks.

Strangely, the sight of him—of Nikolay Kolchak—had a calming effect on me. I overcame all my imagined terrors. This was not to say that I wouldn't be glad to be gone, but I knew now it was just a matter of keeping my nerve. That was it . . . keeping my nerve. Reaching in, I took the coins from my pocket, gripping them hard, while with my other hand I gently peeled back the sacking from the head.

I was relieved that that portion of uncovered face wasn't distinct. Brow, hair, eyes—it might be anyone. Anyone who was dead, that is.

Shrinking away from any contact with the body, I balanced a coin on one closed eye and was ready with the other, telling myself that the moment it was done I would flee that room as if from the presence of the Devil himself. But as I went to put it down I heard a sound. Believing that the old woman had returned, I looked, scowling, towards the door. But the sound hadn't come from outside. My hair began to rise as the truth dawned . . . the sound had come from the dead man.

And then . . . and then . . . in one violent motion its arm threw off the sacking and caught my wrist in a grip that was both cold and sure.

I screamed a soundless scream that tore through my chest and for a moment losing all strength, I collapsed onto the floor. Still the arm did not release me. My heels scrabbled for grip and I punched at it with my free hand, but its grasp never slackened. I heard my coins jangle away into the darkness. And before I could stop it, the corpse rolled onto its side and fell off the table like a solid lump of wood, landing on top of me, crushing the breath from my lungs.

In a frenzy of fear now, I fought against it, but I was trapped whatever I did—pinned down by its heavy unmovable weight.

A sound—a new sound, creeping into my ear. That which had been Nikolay Kolchak was trying to speak.

Exhausted, I lay still, both cold and hot with sweat. Trembling. My stomach knotted in terror.

The creeping whispering sound came again. '. . . Help . . . me . . .'

My voice broke into a wavering sob.

'. . . Ya . . . nis . . . help . . . me . . .'

'Wh-what? How? *How?*' I tried to throw him off. 'Let me go! Let me go!'

'*Shut* . . . up, little fool . . . Help me.'

'How? What do you want from me? How can I help a dead man? *How?* Have mercy, sir. *Please.* Have mercy and let me go. I shall be good. I shall be good. I swear it by all the merciful saints in Heaven.'

By the end my words were meaningless blub-berings.

I heard a hiss of anger.

'Not . . . dead . . .'

'Wh-what?'

'Not . . . dead . . . Alive. *Listen* . . . I need—escape.'

I could feel his weight shifting as he struggled to sit up.

I lay looking up at him, not daring to move. 'But they hung you.'

I watched his hand go to his throat. The cut noose was still there. Slowly and painfully he took it off and dropped it on the floor.

'Hanged . . . yes. Not killed . . . Not killed . . . Believe me.'

'But how?'

'Not ask so many ques-questions . . . Hurt too much, talk.'

251

He was clambering unsteadily to his feet, leaning against the table, his head drooping upon his chest. I suppose I could have run away then, but I didn't.

I sat up, rubbing my wrist. I thought of the Countess and wondered what to do. What would *she* want me to do?

I knew at once.

'If I can help . . . I will . . . you have my word on it. That is . . . tell me what it is I have to do.'

I could hear Nikolay Kolchak swallowing, trying to form his words without pain. I tried to help him.

'Shall I fetch Dr Gomarus? Is that what you want?'

'*No* . . . In forest . . . place. Friends come . . . come for me. Take me there.'

I knew it was wrong of me. I knew he was the Tsar's sworn enemy. But I didn't care.

I stood up and draped his arm around my shoulder.

'You had better lean on me. That's it. I've got you.'

He was heavy, barely conscious; and anyone who saw us emerge from the building might mistakenly believe I was taking home a drunk—an unremarkable sight that night, except that we slipped away quietly into the forest, our way lit by the ghostly luminescence of the Northern Lights, the blue shimmering light coming softly through the trees.

Once into the forest, Nikolay Kolchak rarely spoke, and if he did it was because he had to. He pointed out the path I had to follow, the same one taken each morning by the prisoners on their way to back-breaking labour cutting down trees and hauling them to the sawmill. As soon as we were on it, his head lolled against my shoulder. I think most of the time he slept. And because he relied on me for everything, I found strength for both of us. We were heading deeper into the forest, and if once I lost my way, there would be no hope for us, either we would freeze to death or be picked off by wolves.

But Nikolay Kolchak was my lucky charm, he was the cat with nine lives, and at last we reached a clearing with a small woodcutter's hut at the centre, piles of neatly sawn logs stacked up against its walls. Seeing where we had come to, Nikolay Kolchak roused himself, nodded, then slumped back into a doze.

The hut was deserted, but the fresh provisions that had been left for him made a welcome sight. Quickly I lit a lantern and set about making Nikolay Kolchak as comfortable as possible, wrapping him up in blankets until only his face showed. He was in a wretched way. His skin was grey, and black crusty blood had dried around his nostrils; and when he moved, letting the blankets slip down a little, I was appalled and fascinated in equal measure to see the rope-burn around his neck.

He opened his eyes suddenly and caught me looking at it. I jerked back in surprise, but his bloodshot eyes held my gaze.

'You . . . must go now,' he said.

Go? I looked at him unbelievingly. Was he again trying to dismiss me like his servant? *Go*. After all I had done and risked for him . . . I felt a sense of bitter disappointment welling up inside. It must have shown on my face, but if it did, he didn't comment.

'Yes . . . Friends come. Soon. You go . . . And thank you . . . Thank you.'

'But I—'

'Go . . . Yanis.'

'But—'

'*Go*.'

He spoke as harshly as he was able then grimaced with pain.

I got to my feet and went to the door; looking back I saw him still watching me, willing me to leave.

I nodded curtly and stepped outside, angrily grinding my teeth.

I raced through the forest, still fuming at the unjust way I felt I had been treated. To be so coldly rebuffed when I thought I was his friend. When I thought that Nikolay Kolchak really valued me . . .

I was back at the village more quickly than I would have thought possible.

Its lights shone through the trees.

On entering it and coming round past the church, I found the revelries had abruptly ended. There had been a fight, the wreckage telling its own tale—the broken glass and damaged buildings; the injured being tended by their friends.

The women and children had all fled, and predictably the secret police kept watch from the shadows.

I ran on, my heart tearing at my chest as if to escape. At last I turned into the manor's gateway. The house appeared reassuringly peaceful—the smell of woodsmoke wafting down from the chimneys; oil-lamps burning at unshuttered windows.

Flying up the steps, I raised my fist ready to pound on the door . . . But my arm froze in mid-air . . . then gradually slipped down to my side.

To my surprise I found the door already ajar. This was so far from usual that I hesitated a few moments more before pushing at it with my fingertips, forcing the door to open wide.

The hall. Nothing changed. Mirrors and boots and walking sticks. The bat-plagued bear. But I was already looking past these things. I was looking towards the door of the Countess's drawing-room, seeing that that too stood slightly open.

'Countess?'

I spoke the word breathlessly. My hand went up to my head and pulled off my cap. Clutching it to my stomach, I approached her door.

'Countess?'

Softer now. More controlled. My knock upon the door a timid scratch with my fingernail.

The silence was sinister. The only sound from within the slow ticking of the elephant clock.

'Countess?' I pushed the door at the same time.

With it open, I saw her sitting on the gilded sofa, her back to me, her shoulders perfectly still. Was she asleep? Had the events of the day so thoroughly exhausted her?

Taking several more steps into the room, I saw I was mistaken and that the seated figure was not the Countess at all—it was altogether far too thickset to be her; besides I doubted whether the

Countess would allow herself to be caught napping, whatever the circumstance. A jolt went through me, realizing I was in the presence of Miss Mirsky.

I stood rooted to the spot, not making a sound, wondering if it would be better to turn and sneak away before any harm was done, but something about Miss Mirsky made me curious. Step by step I approached her until I stood at her side.

'Miss Mirsky—are you all right?'

I touched her arm, even then guessing she was dead, her mouth frozen in a grim self-satisfied smile, her eyes neither quite open nor quite closed. Only her watch had any life, any movement—the heart inside *her* cold and still.

Then I noticed a dribble of dark liquid running down from the corner of her mouth—and in her hand she gripped a cup drained to its dregs.

'*Poisoned—she's been poisoned.*'

My voice was barely more than a whisper, and all I could think of was the look of murderous hatred I had seen on the Countess's face.

I backed away, then raced to the Countess's bedroom. Angry now. Bursting in without knocking. For just as I had realized that Miss Mirsky was dead, I knew that the Countess would not be there or anywhere else in the house.

All drawers were pulled open. Clothing scattered on the floor. In haste only bare necessities taken.

With a howl I snatched up a bottle of perfume and dashed it as hard as I could against the wall, the room instantly filling with its overpowering smell and a sense of her.

Almost sick with disgust I retreated to the drawing room. Miss Mirsky smiled her dead smile at me—and at her feet I saw something I had previously overlooked. Her velvet purse. The strings, slightly slackened, revealed the purse's contents. My eyes fixed on the handle of her pistol. Grabbing it up, I rammed it into my coat pocket then flew into the hallway.

'Dr Gomarus! Mrs Kropotkin! Where are you?'

Dr Gomarus came at once, hurrying down from the library, spectacles raised on his forehead, book in hand. He stopped when he saw it was me, peering down at me, puzzled, over the banister. Mrs Kropotkin came puffing out of the kitchen a moment later, tea towel and wet plate in hand. She swivelled her head round.

'What's wrong, dear? Where's the fire?'

Seeing them both unharmed a small murmur of joy arose from my throat. Pointing at the Countess's drawing room, I tried to make them understand.

'In there . . . go see . . . *Go see.*'

'What is it, boy?' asked Dr Gomarus descending several more steps. 'Yanis! Yanis! Wait a minute!'

But I had already fled out of the front door and vanished into the night.

They must have seen me on the forest track—or heard me, for I made no attempt at silence. Not like they did. The first I knew of them was when they rode up alongside me on their horses, trapping me between the flanks of their beasts, which seemed large and menacing close to.

I spun round, striking Kazan's stirruped boot, gazing up at the German Prince. Master as silent as servant, and with every twitch of their mounts, I was buffeted between them.

'So you know too?' I blurted out wildly. 'About Miss Mirsky? About her being murdered?'

The German Prince glanced at Kazan, then lowered his head to speak to me.

'All we know, boy, is that there's much mischief about tonight, and it isn't safe for you to be roaming the forest alone. You had better ride behind Kazan.'

At this, Kazan obediently reached down and hauled me into place, effortlessly lifting me off the ground with just one hand. We set off, me perched as best I could upon the horse's fattened rump, frightened in case I slipped off—sitting stiff and upright and having no feel for the horse's movement. But when I tried to grip Kazan's waist, he knocked my hands aside, making it clear I was to hold on to the back of his saddle.

Soon we were riding at the gallop, the Prince leading, Kazan close behind, and all thoughts of me forgotten. I knew if I fell off I hadn't a hope of either rider stopping. So I held on until my fingers ached; the smell of horse sweat so strong I could taste it. Then the Prince whistled a warning and reined up hard. Leaving the track, he plunged us into territory deep with virgin snow, driving his horse on by repeatedly striking it with his crop. It reminded me of why I disliked him so much, and made me wonder how it was I had managed to fall in with him. More and more I scanned the forest ahead, and as I did, my sense of foreboding grew. For Nikolay Kolchak. For the Countess. For the moment when the Prince found the two of them together.

At last I glimpsed the clearing with the hut at its centre. Outside the door, two lanterns cast star-shaped rays across the snow, and two horses stood tethered nearby.

As we approached, I saw the German Prince unholster his pistol, then followed his gaze.

The Countess had stepped out of the doorway and stood contemplating us with narrowed eyes. Guessing that the game was up for her, she began to make her way towards us, seeming to accept her fate.

Then I noticed she was smiling.

'At last,' she said, greeting the German Prince. 'I was beginning to think you were never going to come.'

That was when I saw his pistol was pointing at me.

At gunpoint I was forced to march across to the hut to witness their preparations to leave, the burden of them falling mostly on Kazan.

For while his master remained mounted, keeping hold of his reins, Kazan strode round to the side and returned with the two other animals. Carefully he helped the Countess onto her white palfrey, then carried Nikolay Kolchak from the hut and lifted him onto the second horse, before tying him into place with ropes. Nikolay Kolchak, now swathed in heavy furs, drifted in and out of consciousness as he sat slumped in his saddle.

All eyes were on him, none on me—the harmless little doctor's boy. Even the German Prince considered me safe enough to reholster his gun. But I would show him, I would show them all . . . Without a word I slowly took out my own pistol and held it before me. Kazan saw it first and flashed a warning to the German Prince, who had to touch the Countess's wrist before she finally—*finally*—lifted her eyes and condescended to look my way. And the Lord be praised, I was happy.

I pointed the pistol at each of them in turn. Kazan, Nikolay Kolchak, the German Prince . . . the Countess.

She did not flinch, but looked pale and elegant on her white mare. I wanted her to shed tears or show an emotion of some kind. Instead she met my eyes with a cold steady resolve.

'You should not have come back here,' she said. 'This is no place for you—not now . . . Ah, but perhaps . . .' A thought crossed her face and she turned and whispered to the German Prince, who reached inside his greatcoat then tossed down several golden coins. They landed in the snow at my feet.

I curled my lip contemptuously, letting the coins lie where they had fallen. Was this what they thought of me—that I would be happy and content with a few crumbs of their gracious kindness? That everything was put right and all past wrongs forgotten? Why was it that their kind always thought the anger of little people didn't count, that we might be bought off if only the price was met? Thinking she had done fair by me, the Countess would no longer look my way, but I could hardly tear my eyes off her. I could feel my anger buzzing inside my head—like bees trapped in their hive—growing louder and louder and—

'*Why, Countess?* Why play such cruel games with me?'

'It is not your place—' began the German Prince imperiously, but the Countess raised her gloved hand to silence him.

'He has a right to know.'

She looked at me defiantly.

'Nikolay Kolchak is my husband. We were married secretly in Koytava ten months ago, and I would do anything in my power to save him.'

'Including killing Miss Mirsky?' I spoke out of shock, for I hardly believed what she had just told me.

She winced, but just then was distracted by Nikolay Kolchak who had started to cough and groan in pain. And I saw in that moment the look of tenderness she gave him, and it maddened me in a way I could not explain.

Instead I focused all my pent-up fury on the German Prince, jabbing my pistol at him.

'And you . . . *you* . . . What kind of man shoots someone on his own side in cold blood?'

He fumbled with his reins.

'It didn't come easy, believe me, but the wretch was a traitor, he had deserted his comrades. If he had reached Osva he might have recognized me and betrayed us all.'

'So you shot him?'

'Yes.'

I shook my head against the buzzing.

'And everything else you did and said—about the Tsar, about revolutionaries—was that just for show? *Was it?* Why, now I come to think about it . . . you're no more a German Prince than I am, are you?'

He half smiled at this and I saw that what I had mistakenly thought of as stupidity and boorishness was in fact slyness and cunning.

'For show . . . ? Yes, it was for show. And making out I was a foolish aristocrat certainly worked on minor officials when getting into a restricted area like Osva. If you must know my real trade, I was a foreman at an iron foundry, burning my hide off for a hundred and fifty draculs a month. That is till I took up the revolutionary cause. You see, it can make good use of a quick-witted fellow like me. I didn't need wealth, or the right family connections, or an education at the military academy. Under Nikolay Kolchak I've risen to second-in-command on my own merit, and I regret nothing. Long live the revolution!'

Towards the end of his speech I was only half listening, growing more aware of Nikolay Kolchak as he again started to cough. When I turned to him, I saw he had opened his bloodshot eyes and was watching me (or more precisely my pistol) and seemed to understand the situation.

'Yanis . . . Come with us . . . Join us . . . Leave your Dr Gomarus . . . Come be a . . . a revolutionary. Forget you were a servant.'

'Leave Dr Gomarus. Are you mad? Why should I want to leave him and join your band of liars? He's the only good man I know. You—you're nothing. You're not fit to breathe the same air as him.'

Nikolay Kolchak closed his eyes, his chest heaving with suppressed coughs. The Countess watched him hawkishly.

'It's too cold for him to be out here, we really must go.'

'No. Not yet. *I'll* tell you when. You haven't answered all my questions yet. If you think—'

Before I realized what was happening, Kazan sprang at me like a leopard and we tussled together with the pistol between us.

He was strong, but I was determined. I gripped the pistol hard.

A muffled shot rang out.

I saw Kazan's eyes flicker wide in surprise.

Immediately I knew what I had done even though I hadn't meant for it to happen.

Stunned I let the pistol drop from my hand into the snow.

Kazan touched his side.

'I'm sorry, Kazan, I'm sorry. It was an accident. God be my witness, it went off—it just went off. I couldn't stop it.'

Blood dripped steadily into the snow—the shot had only grazed him but he was bleeding badly. Despite this, Kazan kept a cool head. Taking advantage of my shock, he quickly overpowered me and dragged me, unresisting, into the hut; there he tied me up and roughly thrust me into a corner.

I stared, horrified, at the blood on my hands and coat, and at Kazan's bloody footprints on the floor.

Then outside I heard a troop of cavalry arrive, and through the open doorway saw that a mounted band of revolutionaries had reined up in the trees along the edge of the clearing. Flank to flank. Nameless grim-faced men on dark steaming horses. Rifles on their backs and sabres at their sides.

Throwing me one last blazing look, Kazan staggered out clutching his wound. He closed the door and I called out after him, begging him not to leave me there in the dark.

But it was the buzzing in my head that really frightened me.

Out in the clearing, I heard voices and the jangle of stirrups as Kazan struggled to mount up. And then, when all were mounted, the small party cantered over to join the main body of horsemen.

'Ho-zahhh!'

From every throat arose the thunderous shout as Nikolay Kolchak was welcomed back by his own. The sound quivered in the air then abruptly fell away into an eerie silence as the revolutionaries wheeled their horses around and melted away into the forest, like spectres from another world.

Alone in the darkness I listened to the terrifying buzzing in my head. A pressure building in my chest as if I would explode. I raged against the ropes that held me down, furiously shouting one moment, whimpering and wailing the next, and calling for the Countess to come to me like an infant for its mother.

And then all at once the buzzing stopped. Still I was hopelessly crying and laughing—for reasons I no longer remembered. But in the silence

deep within me I heard a sound. A strange omin-
ous sound.

Like

a

china

plate

cracking.

I awoke in a strange narrow bunk in a room I did
not know, hot and feverish, every bone in me
aching.

Seeing me stir, Dr Gomarus was immediately
at my side and I was puzzled to see he had grown
a wispy beard that really didn't suit him.

He laid a cold flannel on my brow.

'Better now?'

Weakly I smiled my answer, and as I lay there I
noticed a glass of water on the table beside me
dimple and ripple from tiny vibrations, as if the
room were moving.

'Where am I?' I managed to ask, my voice a dry
and barely recognizable croak.

'Aboard the *Ursus*, Yanis, we're heading back
west.'

He would not allow me to speak any more, but

held up my head from the pillow and helped me take a nasty green potion.

'You have been very ill, child. You suffered a complete nervous and physical breakdown. We found you half frozen in the forest—that was nearly two weeks ago.'

'*Two weeks?*'

'*Shhh.*' He made me be silent and lie still. Besides, I think the potion had a sleeping draught in it. I slipped in and out of a heavy doze, but whether awake or dreaming, I always pictured the same scene in the forest: the four cold-hearted individuals watching me from their horses—the coldest heart of all belonging to the Countess . . .

I might well have thought the whole world as cruel and self-serving as her, had it not been for Dr Gomarus. For under his constant care and supervision I slowly made my recovery, although I never once left my bed in those early days and ate only soup that the doctor had specially prepared for me by one of the ship's restaurants. Once I spilt a little down my chin and suddenly recalled with a shudder of horror the dribble of poison running down from the corner of Miss Mirsky's mouth.

Losing all appetite, I pushed the bowl aside.

Dr Gomarus peered at me over his pink lenses. 'Not hungry?'

'No, not really—but I would like you to sit with me for a while and talk. I have so many things I want to ask.'

Dr Gomarus gave a weary sigh as he came over and sat on the stool by my bed.

'Ah, I knew this hour must come . . . I can't pretend to know all the answers, mind, but there has been enough talk around to enable me to pad out some of the gaps in my knowledge. Mrs Kropotkin, as you can imagine, has had much to say.'

'What's this, doctor? Have you been listening to gossip? And I thought you didn't approve.'

He smiled at my gentle teasing.

'I don't. And it's not the way I'd advise a sensible person to investigate a matter. However needs must . . .'

I struggled to sit up against my pillows, ready to hear what he had to say.

'Tell me first what we are doing aboard the *Ursus.*'

Dr Gomarus shrugged. 'Haven't I mentioned that already? There has been a big clampdown on security at Osva. Our permits were withdrawn at short notice and I was told our presence there was no longer required.'

I opened my mouth to speak, but before I could question him further he said abruptly, 'But

I'd have thought you'd be more interested in the disappearing Countess. I suppose you guessed that she deliberately got herself sent into exile to be close to her husband? You *did* know that Nikolay Kolchak *was* her husband?'

I nodded. 'Yes . . . I found that out—just as I found out that the so-called German Prince had been on their side all the time.'

'I understand from papers found in her room that it rather complicated matters for the Prince when the Countess unexpectedly turned up as she did. Until then his plan had been to storm the prison with the company he had secretly camped out in the forest and to spring Nikolay Kolchak using a mixture of surprise, force, and confusion. But when the Countess arrived and found out, she was having none of it: in her view the plan wasn't sound, especially with the garrison right next to the prison gates. I don't think she had an alternative plan in mind at that stage, but she's an intelligent woman; once she met you the wheels were put in motion.'

'Yes, I allowed myself to be completely taken in by her . . . What a fool I must look.'

'The Countess has made fools out of older and wiser men than you before, right up to ministers of the Tsar. No doubt she will continue to do so to others in the future. You walked into the web she had spun for you and were so blinded by her brilliance you didn't even notice the threads.'

I thought about this for a moment. It was true. Yet it was only now when I looked back that I saw things clearly for what they really were. Then I remembered something which had been bothering me.

'Nikolay Kolchak, he was hanged. Everyone witnessed it. How was it he was still alive afterwards?'

'Ah, I think I've managed to work that one out . . . You remember that icon you took to prison as a gift from the Countess?'

'Yes. In a case—the travelling icon.'

'Well, I suspect it contained more than inspiration for prayers. Indeed, it's my belief it was stuffed full of banknotes. A bribe for the hangman, and Colonel Zhuk, too, I shouldn't be surprised, for I've since heard he's paid off all his outstanding gambling debts and is to be seen strutting around Osva in a smart new uniform.'

'But that hasn't answered my question, doctor— the bribe didn't stop the hanging from taking place, did it?'

'Quite true. But nor was it supposed to. And the lesson Nikolay Kolchak teaches us is how hard it is to kill a man by stringing him up . . . especially if his neck is padded beneath his hood and the drop is shortened and he is cut down with inordinate haste. Now had he faced a firing-squad, well then, that might have proved a more interesting challenge.'

'The Countess would have come up with something,' I said frowning. 'She would have snatched him away from in front of their loaded muzzles.' I gave a wistful laugh. 'And to think I had read the signs so wrong. I thought it was the German Prince who had fallen for her. I thought he was so taken with the Countess that he was sending her secret love letters.'

'Love letters?' Dr Gomarus raised his eyebrows in surprise. 'How can you be so sure they were love letters?'

'I . . . saw one, and he used words like *implore*.'

'I daresay he did, but I wouldn't be so sure he was writing on matters of the heart. Far from it. I think, despite her marriage to Nikolay Kolchak and falling in with the revolutionary cause, the Countess looked down on the Prince somewhat because of his lowly background. No, more likely he was imploring her not to continue her scheme to help her husband. I don't think he approved much of her involvement—or interference, as no doubt he saw it. But the Countess is not one to be easily over-ruled in anything—even if much of that steely determination lies hidden beneath a placid surface. You, dear Yanis, with your prison

273

connections, were a gift to her. I believe she used you precisely because you didn't know what was going on. For that reason she was able to trust you.'

I nodded and said, 'I suppose I should hate her for all the terrible things she has done. I should hate her and Nikolay Kolchak too.'

My voice cracked with emotion.

'*Shh*, there . . . Just be glad that they have gone. Hatred is so taxing and wasteful. It corrodes logical thought. Now let's not speak about this any more. I have a surprise for you. Do you feel well enough to receive some presents?'

'Presents? From who?'

'Why, Mrs Kropotkin and Tonya, of course. Mrs Kropotkin's first.'

He laid something across the bed before me— a pair of hand-knitted socks in blue wool with yellow toes and heels. 'And this is from Tonya—' More carefully he handed me a tin box with a picture of a castle on its lid.

'What's in it?' For some reason I whispered.

'*Cakes*,' came back Dr Gomarus's reply. 'Apparently she baked them especially for you. Hard as rock now, if ever they were soft to begin with, and burnt to a cinder around the edges. *But cakes*. Why, I never saw Mrs Kropotkin look so surprised—she nearly fell down. It seems that when Tonya makes cakes all the flags come out and we must throw our hats in the air. According to Mrs Kropotkin, up to now the only use the girl has ever put the oven to is warming her toes.'

We both laughed at this for it was not much of an exaggeration, and when I opened the tin I saw that the cakes were every bit as unappetizing and inedible as Dr Gomarus had led me to believe.

'Look, there's a note with them,' I said, 'written on the back of one of Mrs Kropotkin's shopping lists.' And picking it up I read aloud: ' "Enjoy them cakes. I hope you get better. I hope you get a nice girl-frend soon. All my love, Tonya"—Look, doctor, how she's spelt "friend".'

'Indeed—and it's good to see your reading has improved to the extent you can point out the mistakes in others.'

I put the note back into the tin and pushed the cakes aside, then I turned to Dr Gomarus with a serious expression on my face.

'Dr Gomarus, there is something you are keeping from me, isn't there? When I asked how we came to be aboard the *Ursus*, you answered so quickly and then changed the subject. And now when I look around I don't see a single piece of your equipment or any of your other important boxes—not one.'

'Ah.'

'Ah? Is that all? Did you think I wouldn't notice or ask? Where is your camera? What has become of it?'

He hesitated as if too embarrassed to tell me. 'Smashed.'

'*Smashed?* How? Who by?'

'The secret police. They arrived the morning after our permits were withdrawn. Five of them. They stamped on all the photographic plates and destroyed every scrap of paperwork. Nothing was spared.'

'Why should they want to do that?'

Again the embarrassed pause.

'I'm afraid, Yanis, they suspected you of being involved in Nikolay Kolchak's escape. It took some doing but eventually I persuaded them you couldn't have been. I pointed out that when you discovered Miss Mirsky murdered, you had gone after the Countess and German Prince with a pistol, and the blood we found on you proved you had put up a fight. Also, if you *had* helped the escape in any way, why did they tie you up and leave you behind? There was no sense in it. Even the Neanderthal policemen came to accept that.'

I listened, appalled. 'But don't you see? I *did* help him, and I knew all the while what I was doing!'

'I know.'

'So because of me and what I did, your great scientific work lies in ruins and will never be finished?'

He smiled serenely. 'The honest truth is, Yanis, it no longer matters.'

I did not believe him. I refused to believe him. Furious, I threw myself down, my face to the wall.

He touched my arm lightly with his fingers.

'No, listen to me, boy, for there is something I have not been truthful with you about. Do you remember Goshka Kulich?'

I half turned, looking back over my shoulder.

'Your old assistant?'

'He never had scarlet fever as I told you. He left me when he discovered what a liability I would soon become—he wanted no part of it.'

I turned to the doctor, giving him my fullest attention again.

'I don't understand.'

Dr Gomarus swallowed and went on, picking his words carefully.

'Goshka Kulich left my service when he found out I have the beginnings of a wasting disease that will eventually kill me . . . There is a long history of it on my mother's side—a family curse, one might say. It starts with a weakening of the eyesight—a certain sensitivity to light—and spreads to other organs until the whole body is affected. So going to Osva was never a good idea in the first place. You see, I was trying to accomplish in weeks what should have taken me years to do. And in any case the early results were proving disappointing and inconclusive. The sad fact is, Yanis, there was nothing there to make my great masterwork out of, and even if there had been, I would never have finished it.'

'So what will you do?'

'While I have my strength there isn't a problem. In Zurich I have a friend from my student days; he's already offered me a teaching post at the university. And there's a little money left over from my family, not much, but it may see me by. As for you, Yanis, you mustn't worry about a thing, I shall take every step to ensure you find suitable employment elsewhere.'

'Elsewhere . . . ?'

I gave a shout, a proper bellow—and, forgetting how ill I'd been, I leapt out of bed and flung my arms around him.

'*No*, I won't hear of it. You think I would leave you after all you have done for me, after you have twice saved me. First from the orphanage, and now this time from prison. Doctor, I owe you everything. Besides, who else will take care of you? Who will shave you in the mornings if not me? And I

can learn to be useful in other ways too. If your
eyesight dims, I'll sit by your side and read to you,
and if you need to write, I'll be there with pen and
paper. *You* are my master. I'll not work for anyone
else. I won't! I'd rather be a beggar on the streets.'

He smiled ruefully and ruffled my hair.

'It means taking on a lot, boy. Think about it,
are you sure—*quite* sure?'

'Of course I am, I've never been more sure of
anything in my whole life.'

Behind his pink lenses I saw his eyes mist with
tears.

'Thank you, Yanis. Thank you. You can't begin
to understand what it means to me to hear you
say this.'

Afterwards I felt much calmer than I had in a long
while, and it made me content just picturing the
days with the two of us together. There would be
dark times too, I realized that, I wasn't stupid. But
I was prepared to meet them as they arose and do
the very best I could.

First, however, I needed my health back. I was
getting stronger almost by the day, and was able
to take a short turn out on deck now, if I didn't

get too cold or tired. It was only when I slept that I knew of the way still to go. I slept deeply and feverishly, often waking soaked in sweat. And I dreamed such vivid dreams that I was never certain if they were 'real' or not.

Once I asked Dr Gomarus which cabin Mrs Kropotkin and Tonya were in.

'Mrs Kropotkin and Tonya?' he repeated, puzzled.

'Yes, Tonya is running away to be a dancer, and Mrs Kropotkin has followed her and is trying to persuade her to return home.'

'But, Yanis, dear boy, they waved us goodbye from the shore at Osva. And as for the notion of Tonya ever earning a living dancing on the stage . . .'

'But Mrs Kropotkin says . . .' My words fell away as suddenly the story struck me as too preposterous ever to have been believable in the first place.

'It must have been a dream, Yanis. That's what it was. A dream.'

'Yes . . . a dream.'

And yet the hold of my dreams remained strong; they were utterly convincing. Then I swore I saw Nikolay Kolchak and the Countess.

It happened while we were docked at Osmabinsk. I was alone and standing at the cabin porthole, which from its far forward position on the ship gave a clear view of the steerage passengers embarking underneath the pier. They came aboard in their usual grey huddle with their animals and bundles and the occasional cart.

At first it was just a mass of people, until my eyes were drawn to a particular couple, the woman helping the man along. To me it was startlingly obvious who they were, despite the Countess being dressed in unflattering peasant clothes and having dyed her hair. Nikolay Kolchak was stooping and slow.

In a moment they had gone from view, but so sure was I of what I'd seen that I started to tremble. I couldn't control myself. I shook so badly that in the end I had to lie down on my bunk and wait for it to pass, and there I fell asleep. I dreamt dream after dream until the doctor woke me, telling me I had been shouting and thrashing my arms and legs. He asked if anything was worrying me, but I couldn't bring myself to tell him. As yet I didn't know if there was anything *to* tell. Dreams and reality—everything had become mixed up in my head, but I was determined to find out the truth.

With the ship now full, we set sail from Osmabinsk and I had to get used to sharing my deck with others. To deal with the increase in passengers, new members of crew had also come aboard, one of whom crossed paths with me a few days later.

'*Oh, hello*—it's you!' I blurted out.

'Sir . . . ?' The steward was polite although clearly he did not recognize me.

'I'm the one you helped before. The doctor's assistant. You let us into steerage to take photographs, remember?'

'Ah yes, sir. Forgive me . . . you look a little changed.'

'Mm . . . I was wondering, that is, can you see your way to letting me down into steerage again?'

He drew back a little.

'I don't know about that, sir. Not now. It was different before, but ever since that nastiness up at Osva . . .'

'*Please*. Just this once. I'll not breathe a word of it to anyone.'

He hesitated, weighing up the matter, looking at my pleading face.

'Oh . . . very well. This way, sir—take care not to let anyone see.'

The climb down the steps exhausted me. He waited patiently at the bottom.

'You know what to do, sir? How to come back up?'

I nodded, leaning against the side.

'You are quite sure about this, sir, aren't you? If I may say so, you don't seem at all well.'

'I'm fine, really I am.'

Brushing his concerns aside, I waited for him to unlock the door. He opened it a fraction and I slipped by giving a nod of thanks.

The door shut quickly behind, leaving me alone to face the seething cavernous deck. I had forgotten the distinct sights and sounds and smells of steerage. Now they hit me all at once, rocking me back on my heels, especially the smell—a rank mixture of wood-smoke, sweat, and manure.

I moved forward, my senses battered by the roaring crowds, my eyes flitting from face to face, my feet leaden, following the endless flow of people.

'. . . and watch my hands, good sir, watch my hands. Did you ever see such artful fingers? No, don't blink, sir, if you do you'll miss it. It's all a matter of concentration.'

Eventually I found myself part of a big crowd gathered round to watch a trickster fleece a group of squaddies. A small collapsible table had been set up, and the soldiers were taking turns to guess where a dice was, each time placing their bet before one of three cups.

'That one. It has to be—'

'Wrong again, my friend. See—? At this rate you'll never make a general.'

The trickster clawed in the money and the soldier was shoved aside by his friend, who showed he was ready for another game by squatting down low to the table and spitting into his palms.

'Follow my hands, good sir, follow my hands . . .'

Like the others I watched, rapt, but not the game, which I couldn't care less about. Instead I found my gaze riveted elsewhere. I edged round for a better view, growing impatient with those who blocked my way yet using the crowd for cover. From it I observed the Countess, seeing her kneel at Nikolay Kolchak's side—

'That one!' declared the soldier, and the crowd surged forward to see if he was right.

She seemed tired and her once glorious hair was hacked shapeless and stained red. But she was still beautiful. Rising, she picked up a bucket and, speaking a few words to Nikolay Kolchak, went to fetch water. She passed a group of soldiers. They leered at her and turned to each other with gap-toothed grins. In her absence, Nikolay Kolchak dozed.

Watching him closely, I pushed forward until at last I stood before him. I didn't make a sound, but sensing someone there, he opened his eyes. He showed no surprise that it was me.

'Yanis . . . forgive me if I do not rise.'

I said nothing.

Wearily he lifted his eyes to me again.

'I believe in chess this would be the closing moment. Checkmate. There is nowhere else I can go. You have me cornered, Yanis.'

Still I saw no need to speak, but hearing a sharp gasp and a crash, turned my head. The Countess had come back, dropping the bucket at the sight of me and soaking her dress. She dashed past to be at Nikolay Kolchak's side.

'What are you doing here? Why don't you leave us alone?'

'That's good coming from you,' I said coldly. 'I see you everywhere, even in my dreams, Countess.'

'*Shh—shh*. You mustn't call me that. How did you know where to find us?'

'I saw you come aboard at Osmabinsk. I picked you out straight away. But why take the risk?'

The Countess glanced at her husband. He smiled back at her, unconcerned; she spoke quietly as if to him, her hand stroking his hair.

'Nikolay couldn't manage the journey on horseback. He gradually grew sicker. We thought—*I* thought we could slip by. In disguise. I thought we could stay with sympathizers until he was well enough to rejoin his men. I never expected . . .' She looked up at me. 'What do you intend to do now, Yanis? Hand us over and claim the reward?'

A rush of anger brought a bitter taste to my mouth. *Money once again*—didn't she understand me at all? But then more clear-headedly I wondered about it. The doctor—the one genuinely good man I knew—would need money to make his last years comfortable. He would need medicines and surgeons—in the end a decent funeral too. Money was bound to be tight. Much tighter than he had considered.

I shrugged.

Then Nikolay Kolchak began to cough. The Countess wouldn't leave his side but kept glancing anxiously at the bucket of water. I picked it up and carried what was left of it across, and kneeling beside Nikolay Kolchak I took out the tin cup sunk at the bottom. Gently I cradled his head, lifting the cup to his lips. He drank and closed his eyes.

'Thank you, Yanis.'

Slowly I stood up and began to back away.

The Countess flew at me, plucking at my sleeve.

'Is that it? You mean to go without another word . . . ? You can't, I won't let you. Not without first telling us what you intend to do. Tell us, I say.'

She grew almost wild.

'Everyone is looking at you. Is that what you want?'

'Oh, but my dear, sweet Yanis—'

'*Stop it.* I am not your dear, sweet anything.' I struggled to hold back my emotions.

'No . . . no, quite so. I see that now.'

Her hand slowly fell away.

'You have grown up in these past few weeks, Yanis. You don't seem quite the child you were.'

'You tend to grow up fast when you've been through what I have,' I said laughing bitterly.

'That was never our intention, Yanis. *Never.* You know that's true. And now . . . ? If you have any love left for us, any at all, I beg you to consider—'

'I don't know what I am going to do! I'm tired . . . I can't think straight. *Just leave me alone.*'

I turned abruptly and walked away, losing myself in the crowd. I did not look back; I knew she would be watching.

The steward came when I pushed the bell, his beaming smile and chirpiness oddly out of place.

'You get all your business settled, sir?'

'Yes. There's no need for me to go down there again.'

I followed him up the stairs, the air bitingly fresh. At my side he babbled on, but I didn't listen to a single word.

I allowed myself a secret nod.

I had made my decision.

Stephen Elboz started to write because he liked day-dreaming, and to him writing was the next logical step. He wrote his first novel in secret at his junior school in Wellingborough, Northants although he now admits it was terrible. Fortunately he was encouraged to persevere by one of his teachers. Whilst at Lancaster University, he won a writing competition and had a play produced on the local radio station.

Stephen divides his time between writing and teaching at a junior school in Corby, Northants. He tries to encourage his pupils to develop their skills and enjoyment of writing in the same way he was encouraged by his teacher at school. Stephen's first book, *The House of Rats*, won the Smarties Young Judges Prize for the 9–11 age category.

Other books by Stephen Elboz

Kit and his best friend, Prince Henry,
spend wonderful nights flying across
London on Kit's magic carpet,
looking for adventure—and they find it!

But when Prince Henry falls into terrible
danger, it's up to Kit to rescue him.
He must brave the horrors of the tunnels
beneath London and defeat the evil
Stafford Sparks. But will his magic
be strong enough?

ISBN-13: 978-0-19-275134-8
ISBN-10: 0-19-275134-4

STEPHEN ELBOZ

A Land Without
Magic

'Nobody does it better than Elboz –
and that includes J.K Rowling herself' *The Guardian*

The wicked Stafford Sparks has escaped
from prison, and he's coming after Kit!
Kit must flee the country at once, so he and
Prince Henry travel to the tiny land of
Callalabasa.

But too late Kit discovers that in this
remote country, magic is forbidden and
evil lurks around every corner. Are Kit and
Henry really out of danger here,
in a land where enchantment is
banished and the League
Against Magic are plotting to
destroy the country?

ISBN-13: 978-0-19-275199-7
ISBN-10: 0-19-275199-9

A wild kind of magic has arrived . . .
there's a killer on the loose . . . and a new,
mysterious plant is coming to life. For Kit
these are just the right ingredients for
adventure and he's determined to
be a part of it.

He and Prince Henry fly across London
trying to find out just what's going on.
American Indians, vampires, Moonweed,
Jack the Ripper . . . surely the evil
Stafford Sparks must have a hand
in all this somewhere?

ISBN-13: 978-0-19-275265-9
ISBN-10: 0-19-275265-0

Kit's father's disappeared. In the middle of
the ocean—just gone without a trace. And
that's not all—boats, ships, and even
whole islands are vanishing into thin air.
Kit and Prince Henry are off on
another adventure.

As they set off on Kit's flying carpet they have a
sneaking suspicion that their old adversary,
Stafford Sparks, may have a hand in all the
strange goings-on. And when they reach a
mysterious island, in the middle of the ocean,
they realize that it's not just Kit's father that's in
terrible danger—it could be the entire world.

ISBN-13: 978-0-19-275343-4
ISBN-10: 0-19-275343-6